Sleeping Dogs

William Paul

1

The naked man went down on his knees in front of the hissing gas fire, so close to it that the richly pink colouring of his flesh seemed to be sucked to the front of his body leaving his back a pallid ghostly white. He kept his spine erect, bowing his head to rest his chin on a platform of intertwined fingers. A bright silver chain was wrapped twice round the knuckles of his right fist. The crucifix it was attached to was hidden inside the two hands, cupped between the palms like something alive and delicate awaiting release.

In the warm darkness of the curtained room he prayed silently. His lips moved rapidly but no words emerged. As he prayed his forehead creased with wrinkles and he pressed his hands more tightly together. The sharp edges of the crucifix gouged into his skin, causing him discomfort. Familiar feelings of guilt and shame popped up in his mind but distantly, like faraway targets rising and falling on a firing range. He squeezed his hands more tightly until the discomfort turned into actual pain and then he squeezed harder still.

Abruptly he stopped praying and opened his eyes. Someone else was entering the room behind him. He did not move. He did not turn his head. He remained kneeling, staring into the yellow and white flames pouring upwards over the red-hot fireclay towers. The heat was severe against his eyeballs and it flowed down the front of his body like a layer of molten plastic sticking to the contours of his body.

Behind him, where his flesh prickled in the comparative coldness, he could sense movement. He could hear the softest of footsteps on the carpet and the faint electric crackle of static. A grotesquely distorted human reflection rippled fleetingly across the dull beaten copper of the fire surround.

He tensed as a hand touched his left shoulder. An inner emptiness expanded up and around him as if he had just stepped off a cliff. His whole body was on fire now. He was soaking up the heat like a sponge. Droplets of sweat seemed to block every pore, squeezing out reluctantly like toothpaste from a near-empty tube.

The hand patted and stroked his bare flesh. It moved slowly down over his chest, sliding smoothly over the hairs. He saw the blood-red fingernails, like the heads of exotic snakes, glide all the way down to his stomach. Another hand touched his right shoulder. More scarlet fingernails brushed gently at the other side of his chest. Strong sweet perfume made his nostrils flare. A gently yielding softness pushed against his back, a gossamer veil of hair fell over his eyes so that he was totally enveloped from head to toe in the most sensuous warmth.

'Are you ready for me yet, Donald?' a purring feminine voice whispered hoarsely in his ear. 'Have you asked for your forgiveness before we get started?'

Father Donald Byrne was a big, powerfully built man. There was thick dark hair on his chest and shoulders. He closed his eyes and squeezed the sharp-edged crucifix savagely. The sweat was running freely over his face and chest. His whole body trembled.

He stood up and turned to step into the inviting female embrace, burying his face in the woman's long hair and kissing her neck to feel the arterial pulse of warm blood against his lips. He unwound the chain from his fingers and dropped the crucifix. It hit the floor soundlessly as he picked up the woman effortlessly and carried her towards the bedroom. Through the door he could see that the covers on the bed were pulled down in readiness. Despite moving away from the fire, his body still burned furiously. Desire and anticipation made him breathe heavily, made his movements clumsy. Spittle bubbled at the corners of his mouth. The red-tipped fingers clawed impatiently, vindictively at his back. Her teeth nipped the flesh of his breast. The darkness intensified as he kicked the bedroom door shut with his heel and dropped the clinging woman from waist-height on to the bed.

He hesitated momentarily, looking down at the woman sprawled below him. The saliva was thick in his throat, so thick he could hardly swallow it to be able to breathe. The demon lust made him tense and hard. He bent down towards her. The fingernails reached up and hooked into his shoulder blades.

'Forgive me, Lord,' he murmured in words that floated out on exhaled breath. 'Forgive me, for I know exactly what I am about to do.'

2

The shivering junkie stood in the centre of the room while Gus Barrie kept his back to him as he played the pinball machine. Lights flashed, music stuttered, an intelligible computer voice gabbled loudly, and the scoring digits spun into the millions. When the steel ball jumped off a bumper at an angle and cracked loudly against the underside of the glass the junkie winced as if it had hit him in the head. Barrie went on playing.

Ross Sorley hugged his arms round his thin body and rocked from side to side. Withdrawal was hurting him. It was scraping at the inside of his brain and making his blood run too fast. His eyes were puffy and swollen and his teeth felt strange, as if they were barely attached inside his mouth and floating about loosely. He needed a hit and he needed it very badly. Every vein where he had ever stuck a needle was wasp-sting sore. He desperately needed to be stung again.

When Barrie's heavies had lifted him off the street he had offered only token resistance. The Jones brothers were evil bastards who enjoyed their work. They were muscle-bound giants with near-shaven heads containing tiny brains. There was no point in arguing with them or fighting them. They only hit him once, once each, both at the same time, a slap on the side of the head and a hard punch to the stomach. Then Billy pushed his face into the back seat of their car and sat on him while delivery was made. It was all relatively painless. He was grateful for the small mercy.

Junkies like Sorley didn't frighten easily. Fear was for rational people who cared if they lived or died. He was too far gone, too hopeless a case. Even though he had spent the previous two weeks in hiding because he had heard a whisper that Barrie was after him, he was glad to be found. Barrie was a businessman. When he realised Sorley really was not in a position to settle the debt they would negotiate. Promises would be made, a deal would be cut. It had happened before. It would happen again.

He had been standing watching Barrie play pinball at the middle machine in a row of five for fifteen minutes. There was a snooker table on one side of him and multigym equipment beyond it. Sandy Jones had stripped down to vest and shorts and was pumping some iron on a bench. Billy was a menacing invisible pain behind him.

Sorley was aware of the glass wall on his other side that separated the room from the swimming pool under its opaque glass roof. The moving reflection of the water's surface on the ceilings and walls was annoying and sore on his eyes. He dimly remembered standing in the same spot many years before. It had been so different then. He had been smartly dressed, clear-headed, sharp as a knife. He and Georgie Craig had been discussing going into partnership with Barrie. A different time. A different world.

The pinball machine suddenly blared out a trumpet fanfare and the computerised voice boomed out a hard luck message. The lights went out. Gus Barrie slapped the sides and turned to face Sorley. A look of displeasure transformed slowly into one of distaste.

'Ross, look at yourself.'

Sorley took the command literally. He opened out his arms and looked down at the dirty grey T-shirt, the torn jeans, and the trainers with string for laces. When he looked up again Barrie's fist exploded in his face.

'What a fucking mess you are, Ross. You wanted to play with the big boys but instead of getting smart you got a habit. You stupid pathetic bastard.'

Sorley was hauled back to his feet, blood dribbling from his mouth. He spat out a broken tooth and stared at it on the floor. 'Sorry, Gus,' he said, remembering that he had once owned a silver Porsche. And a genuine Swiss watch that cost more than five thousand pounds. He felt his wrist to check that it was gone.

'You knew my brother, so I gave you a chance and you screwed up. I'm too sentimental. I'm just too fucking sentimental.'

Barrie shook his head. Sorley nodded. He hadn't known the younger brother, Mike Barrie, very well at all. Had met him a few times, drank with him in a club once, had fancied his wife. Who wouldn't? He was called Mad Mike because he was a nutter, completely psycho and probably clinically insane. A dangerous bastard, but only to himself in the end as it turned out. Sorley, back from a few years in America, had dropped the name to get restarted and had teamed up with Georgie Boy who had an inside track with the Barrie clan. Mad Mike was dead and couldn't argue. Gus Barrie, who had taken on the running of the family business after Mike's death, had been impressed. People had thought Gus was too soft to run the business, too emotional. They were wrong. A different time. A different world.

'Are you listening to me?' Barrie asked, frowning slightly. 'I'm expecting a lady shortly, you see, Ross. A very classy lady. That's why I need the money. I owe the money to her. I promised to pay it back and she's coming over to collect it.'

Sorley swayed and frowned, matching his expression to Barrie's. He had owned a woman once, long legs, big breasts, perfect teeth, fingernails like claws, flawless skin. A truly beautiful woman.

'I can't allow it, Ross. If one gets away without paying, why should any of the others feel an obligation? I can't let you back on the street. You're bad for business, Ross.'

'But I'm just a junkie.'

'Sorry, Ross.'

'I've no money.'

'I know. You've no future either.'

Barrie turned and walked away along a long curving corridor. Automatic sensors in the walls switched the lights on ahead of him as he walked along and switched them off behind. Soft music followed him too, a female's sweetly hoarse voice whispering words of love.

Sorley stood where he was, still frowning in puzzlement as he watched Barrie's broad shoulders and thick arms dwindle in the moving bubble of light and music. He couldn't make sense of what was happening. He took a step forward, wanting to follow, reaching out, wanting to explain. But a hand grabbed his outstretched arm. Billy Jones was in front of him, blocking the way.

'Go to hell,' Sorley said angrily.

'After you, smackhead,' Billy replied and pushed him in the chest.

Sorley did not see the twelve-inch length of razor wire that Sandy Jones looped over his head from behind. He felt it, though, as the blades sliced cleanly through the outer skin of his throat causing a dozen tiny wasp stings of pain. An instant later the artery had been torn open and blackness bubbled up to cloud his eyes. It mixed with the tinny echoing music and flashing lights from the pinball machine.

Sorley wasn't afraid. He didn't even struggle. He smelled the leather seats of his silver Porsche and the perfumed body of his beautiful woman. Within a matter of seconds he was dead.

3

The bath water was so hot it took David Fyfe's breath away. He lowered himself through the thin layer of soapy bubbles slowly, enduring the infuriatingly itchy tingling sensation caused by the oily liquid against his skin because he knew it would not last more than a few seconds. When he finally lay down, stretching out to his full length, only his head was visible with his chin resting on the surface. His entire body was wrapped tightly in a winding-sheet of hot water. He thought he was releasing a quietly satisfied sigh but it came out more like an astonished gasp.

Detective Chief Inspector Fyfe was greatly irritated by the thought of going in to work the next morning. There were so few hours between then and now. So little time to rest. So little time to himself. The treadmill was turning and he had to keep pace with it or suffer the consequences.

It was a pity he needed to earn money to live on. He had no savings, no capital except for the heavily mortgaged house and the equally heavily mortgaged flat in the city that Sally had bought when they were living apart. The rent from the flat paid that mortgage, but the latest tenants had just left and it had become a liability again. He and Sally were back together again and she didn't have a job. If he stopped working, he stopped earning and, in the worst case scenario, he stopped eating. It might not be true, but it was the way his mind was programmed. The Calvinist work ethic had been dinned into him as a child in a relatively poor family doing his milk round in the morning and his paper round at night. He had always worked, always had a regular income and good money. He was a wage slave grown so used to the chains he was terrified of what might happen if they were ever broken.

Fyfe lifted both his arms out of the water. He wiped them dry with a towel and picked up the glass of malt whisky on the edge of the bath beside his head. He had placed it there before immersing himself. The ritual of the hot bath and the good whisky had served him well over the years. It was a soothing influence that rarely failed to calm him and restore his equanimity when things began to get on top of him. A womb substitute.

His work with the Fraud Squad had been frustrating him horribly for the last month. Cases going round in circles, getting nowhere. Every night he came home with a sore back and stiff neck from hunching over files and accounts that were like a foreign language to him. That afternoon he had spent four hours with a bunch of tax inspectors and accountants trying to decide if some fat rich bastard had committed a crime or not. The answer had been a reluctant no.

Fyfe wanted his old job in the mainstream CID back. He needed to meet real people, catch real criminals. But they didn't want him back. They didn't want him there at all, that was why he had been shunted sideways into Fraud and passed over when the last superintendent's post had fallen vacant. He had too much of an extra-curricular track record to be a serious candidate, though he hadn't given up hope until another less controversial name was posted on the noticeboard. Sometimes he thought it was a miracle he ever got to DCI level. He must have been good at his job, must have enjoyed it at some stage. It was just that he couldn't remember when.

Fyfe sipped the whisky and closed his eyes. Wednesday night, he thought. Only two days to go before the weekend. He shifted lazily in the luxurious warmth and the latent heat tightened its grip, warning him to remain motionless. He imagined that every pore in his body was gaping wide open and the bath water was filling him up. He had been born too late, he thought drowsily. He should have been a Victorian gentleman with a country estate and independent means. Having to work for a living was rather vulgar, after all.

The phone started ringing. He assumed Sally would answer it. The bubbles were evaporating rapidly on the bath's surface, leaving a film of white that separated into a dozen different islands. Steam rose upwards in columns like unravelling strands.

The phone was still ringing. He remembered that Sally was out on the hill walking the dogs. Fyfe had to climb out of the bath, grab a towel and go through to the bedroom. Damp footprints darkened the carpet.

'Hello?'

'David, is that you? Sir Duncan here.'

Fyfe hesitated, suspecting a hoax. Sir Duncan Morrison, the Chief Constable, phoning him at home so late at night? Something was wrong.

'David, I hoped to catch you at home.'

It was Hunky Dunky. The inflection in the voice was unmistakable. It really was him. What was it all about? Something was wrong.

'I just wanted to check you would be around tomorrow. I want to see you first thing.'

'Yes, I'll be there.'

'Good. I've got a little job that needs doing. It's something a bit off the beaten path. You're the man I need.'

Hunky Dunky had saved Fyfe's career when he had been struggling with woman and drink problems. He had given him a chance and Fyfe had taken it. The penalty was never being fully trusted again. So what was this little job? Hunky Dunky knew Fyfe owed him. He knew Fyfe would do what he wanted. Whatever it was.

'Very intriguing, sir.'

'I'll see you first thing, then.'

Fyfe put down the phone and hurried back to the bathroom. He pushed the white net curtain to one side and looked out. The sky glowed with its cargo of stars but at ground level the darkness of the countryside was total. The trees and the hills were all hidden in it. The only things visible were the elongated raindrops streaking through the faint light thrown from the window. A blustery wind rattled the frame and shattered brittle dead leaves against the glass. Fyfe shivered and sought the sanctuary of his hot bath.

4

John Adamson, known to his friends as Jad, lay on his back on the top bunk and stared out through the cell window at a strangely dark-pale sky. A sparse sprinkling of stars was spread unevenly among the round-cornered rectangular shapes formed by the pattern of bars. The stars shone weakly, at times seeming to flicker and fade like tiny flames being snuffed out, but never seeming to grow any fewer in number.

Out of sight below the stars, Adamson knew, were the lights of the city of Edinburgh. He had stood by cell windows in different prisons often enough by night over the last nine years looking out, sometimes catching glimpses of distant people hurrying about the streets. He imagined himself into their living-rooms and bedrooms, imagined himself leading a normal life with kids to send to school in the mornings and a job to go to during the day. He invented boring conversations between husbands and wives and passionate whispers between adulterers. He created an entire fantasy town inside his head and took his own place at the centre of it, observing everything that went on around him.

That fantasy world seemed more real to him than his actual surroundings when he was allowed out on his training-for-freedom days and weekends, and nearly always he was glad to get back behind the solid barrier of the prison's high fence and into the welcoming familiarity of his little cell with its window on to his own private world.

Soon, however, he would be out for good. Out after nine long years of captivity. It had been a long time and recently the passing of the weeks and days had seemed to deliberately slow down just to mock him. The end was in sight at last. His parole had been authorised, signed and sealed. It would be good to be a free man again.

The prospect excited and terrified him in equal measure. He craved his freedom but hated the idea of stepping outside the routine he had structured his life round for so long. He was worried about old enemies with long memories who had the advantage of being part of the world he was just joining again. But it was going to happen, whether he liked it or not. He had no choice. He was going to have to let go of the side and push out where his feet did not touch the bottom. Then it was sink or swim. He was as old as his highest ever snooker break, thirty-two, and he had learned his lesson. Next time he would not get caught.

Adamson had a Rizla packet and a tin box of tobacco balanced on his chest. He rolled himself a thin cigarette and drew the edge of the paper over his tongue. The end flared brightly when he used the throwaway gas lighter. The walls of the cell soaked up the brief spasm of light. Tiny flames ate hungrily at the paper until they reached the guts of the cigarette and settled to a red glow. Flakes of charred, black paper floated down on to his bare skin.

Charlie Morris, another failed armed robber, who occupied the bottom bunk in the cell, punched the bottom of the mattress. 'What's the matter, neighbour?' he said. 'Can't get to sleep thinking about all the havoc you're going to create outside once they let you go?'

'Right first time,' Adamson replied.

'Pass us down a fag then, Jad, and I'll keep you company.'

Without looking, Adamson let his arm hang down. He felt fingers take hold of the small cigarette. Once it was gone he began packing another paper full of tobacco from the tin. Poor Charlie, he thought. Another year at least for him to serve. Adamson smiled contentedly at his good fortune.

'A penny for your thoughts,' Morris said.

'The bidding will have to start a lot higher than that.'

'You're a lucky bastard, Jad,' Morris said. 'Everything arranged for you. A flat and a job to go to. Who says crime doesn't pay?'

'Everything comes to him who waits, Charlie. Keep the faith and you'll be all right.'

From his bunk Adamson stared at the star-speckled night sky beyond the bars. Now that he was so close to freedom the recurring images of events that had deprived him of it kept playing in a continuous mind game inside his head; the ambush of the truck by him and his partner Mad Mike Barrie, the astonished faces of the security guards, the unexpected weight of the banknotes and the sheer exhilaration of counting the money. One million, three hundred and seventy-eight thousand, two hundred and fifty pounds, all of it in used, untraceable notes destined for incineration. It was a nice round number once they had used the surplus fivers to buy a Chinese carryout and to light celebration cigars.

It couldn't last, of course. It went from there to the guttering candle, oily to the touch, and the sharp, eye watering smell of petrol. Then came the chase across the city and the wailing sirens and crackling megaphones and flashing blue lights, punctuated by the gunshots before the final explosion and the blood plopping like fat raindrops on the top of his head as it dripped from the ceiling. Every time he thought about it he could feel the warm spots break out on his scalp. Every time, he reached up and ran his hand over his head to convince himself it was only his imagination.

By comparison with the robbery and the arrest, the trial seemed to have been conducted in slow motion. The judge was a fat man, sitting behind a red-draped bench in front of shelves of books. His head was perched on top of a pyramid of red and white robes and his black bushy eyebrows settled low on his forehead.

Adamson remembered his voice most acutely. It had flowed like treacle, the words seeming to queue up in his throat, each waiting its turn to be released and to fall ponderously from his mouth. Adamson believed he had performed well, sticking religiously to his story that he was very much the youthful apprentice, on a salary for his part in the raid rather than a share of the proceeds. Mad Mike had been the boss, the unstable criminal genius who preferred to blow his brains out rather than go to prison. Adamson was the boy from a deprived background, taken advantage of by criminal elements but basically harmless and ready to follow the straight and narrow now that he had learned his lesson. Mad Mike's brother paid for a good lawyer who made him sound more sinned against than sinning.

He was not surprised at the jury's guilty verdict but he was shocked at the length of sentence he received. Twelve years when his QC had promised three at the most. Old bastard must have got out of the wrong side of bed this morning, the QC said unhelpfully afterwards.

The sentence was upheld on appeal and Adamson was convinced its severity was related to his stubborn refusal to agree that the money was still out there somewhere. There were all sorts of rumours. The police told him they believed it had somehow been smuggled out of the country to Mad Mike's widow Angela, who had fled to Spain a week after his death. The original trial judge certainly thought Adamson knew more than he was telling.

Not a day went by in prison without Adamson thinking of that judge. Maybe he wasn't as stupid as he looked, all dolled up like a wee lassie playing dressing-up games with granny's clothes. The man dominated his thoughts even more than the money. Inside prison, Adamson soon realised few people were prepared to believe his story either. Everybody assumed he had his share stashed away as a pension fund and, since it gave him a certain celebrity status, he never denied it outright. He didn't admit to it either. He allowed the legend to grow. It gave him self-respect. It was his secret and he guarded it jealously.

'Mike went daft,' Adamson had told a hushed courtroom during the trial. 'He was battering his head off the walls. He kept firing the shotgun through the window, loading it again and again until he only had two cartridges left. Then he turned on me and I thought I was dead. "They're not going to take me alive, Jad," he said, "I'd rather be dead."'

Adamson had spent weeks carefully composing the story of what went on during the siege, rehearsing every last detail to make himself word perfect. But once he began telling it he had to bite the inside of his lip to stop himself laughing. It was so melodramatic and over the top. They're not going to take me alive, Mike had said like a bad actor on speed. He fully expected them to laugh at him, to shake their heads impatiently and demand to know the real truth. But they didn't. They listened solemnly and they apparently believed him. The newspapers had lapped it up, relating it in screaming headlines. The reporters wrote it as if they had been present in the barricaded room as events unfolded so rapidly, adding an extra layer of authenticity. They conveyed so well the tension and the fear and the panic and the everlasting image of Barrie, suddenly calm, standing in the centre of the room.

'There's no way out, Jad,' Mad Mike said quietly. 'We're cornered but they're not going to take me alive. Why don't you follow me? Don't worry. It's not so hard to die.'

And he put the barrels of the shotgun in his mouth and blasted the top of his skull off. The lead shot had flowered upwards and outwards, splattering the ceiling and walls with a scarlet circuit diagram of how Barrie's blood and brains and bones had all fitted together. Adamson had been staring at it open-mouthed when the police burst into the room.

Adamson grinned. He swung his legs off the bunk and sat up to light his cigarette before slipping to the floor. On his first night of imprisonment at Peterhead he remembered looking out the cell window and down across the wide bay where a clutch of long-backed oil supply boats circled their moorings in the shadow of the huge structure of a drilling rig in for repair hard up against the breakwater. Beyond the boats was a tight huddle of grey houses by the edge of the sea. In those houses his fantasies had taken root.

'Not long now, Jad,' Morris said from below. 'Remember to send me a postcard.'

Adamson sniffed. A tiny sliver of unreality forced its way into his thoughts. His guts hardened like setting concrete. Suppose, it suggested, you've been tricked. Suppose Mike Barrie didn't burn the money. Or suppose it did find its way to the grieving widow in Spain. How she must have been laughing at him these last nine years. How she must have laughed.

On his away days from prison he had passed the scene of the crime a hundred times, smelling again the petrol fumes, seeing again the innocent candle flame casting its dancing shadows over the bundles of notes. It was impossible. Mike Barrie could not have achieved such a thing. And yet, like the prisoners who thought he was hiding the truth, perhaps the truth had been hidden from him. What a brilliant secret that would be.

'You will learn that the world owes you nothing,' the judge had said, black eyebrows quivering. 'Everything in this life has to be paid for, one way or another.'

In the cell, Adamson shook his head as though bothered by a troublesome fly. He was looking forward to his release. Freedom was a seductive creature. Once he was out for good he would be able to find out if he had been tricked. But he had promised himself it was not true and that his secret remained as fresh as ever. It had become an article of faith, a certainty, a promise that could not conceivably be broken.

'Cross my heart,' Adamson murmured, unaware that he was tracing the tip of a forefinger over his chest. 'And hope to die.'

5

The rough surface of the old tarmac road leading down to the beach at Portobello petered out into the sand. Gus Barrie reversed the battered blue Ford Transit van slowly through the shadows of the empty buildings on either side. He stopped as soon as the rear wheels showed signs of sinking in.

'Dump him,' he said, putting the van into first gear and keeping his foot on the clutch.

In the back of the van Billy and Sandy Jones moved awkwardly in the cramped space. Close up, they were hard to tell apart. At a distance it was impossible. The only real distinguishing features were the lion head tattoos on their necks, Billy's on the left side, Sandy's on the right. And the single gold hoop ear-rings, Billy's on the right, Sandy's on the left. But it didn't matter which was which anyway. They were as dumb as cattle, loyal as puppies, biddable muscle on the hoof that helped to keep Barrie ahead of the game. When he whistled, they were always ready to jump.

The inside door handle on the back doors was stiff and had to be thumped hard to make it open. The dull ringing of the metal sounded unnaturally loud in the dark silence of the street. The brothers heaved their burden to the edge and looked over their shoulders for final confirmation.

Barrie saw the scene in the rear-view mirror. He was warm in his thick sheepskin coat, oblivious to the cold wind buffeting the van and leaking in through the ill-fitting windows. A thin film of rain laced the air outside, covering the windscreen in a pattern of tiny dots. They had been sitting in the van in the street for half an hour to be sure it was safe. It was deserted. Nothing moved. The tenements lining it on both sides were derelict, soon to be demolished to make way for a new road. Ancient shop frontages that once attracted the custom of seaside visitors were boarded up. Flaking paint under the dim street lights still conveyed a few faded messages for ice cream and hot dogs. The tattered remnants of a red and white canopy flapped pathetically against the wall. In the distance on the curve of Portobello Bay the tops of the chimneys of the power station were lost in an opaque mass of low cloud.

Barrie's breathing was fast and shallow. Soon Angie would be back, he kept thinking. Soon Angie would belong to him, body and soul. It had taken him so long to achieve it, he hardly dared believe that it was now so close. He just had to get this business finished with. Tidy up the last few loose ends. Then it would be just him and Angie, just like he had always planned.

'Okay, boss?' Billy Jones asked.

The image in the rear-view mirror snapped into focus for Barrie. 'Yes, yes,' he said. 'Dump him quick.'

'Our pleasure.'

Ross Sorley's lifeless body splashed down into the soft sand with barely a sound. The head, wrapped in a Safeway plastic bag, lay at an impossible angle along an outstretched arm. The sand started to darken around it as blood oozed out.

The doors of the van creaked shut and the Jones brothers returned to their seats on the inside wheel hubs. The van pulled away on to the firm tarmac, moving unhurriedly. Sorley's body behind quickly merged into the obscurity of the sand.

Barrie fought his impatience to keep the van's speed down. Everything would soon be in place and perfect. It wasn't going to be fouled up now. He had attended to every last detail, worked out every possible combination of circumstances. There was risk, huge risk involved, but all life was a risk. Barrie had grown to like it that way.

'Someone will get a nice surprise come the morning,' Billy Jones said and Sandy giggled like a girl.

In the mirror Barrie saw the silvery reflection of the moonlight on the sea. He frowned a little although he didn't know why when he saw that it was impossible to tell where the water ended and the sky began.

6

Head down, legs and arms pumping hard to maintain forward momentum on the steep slope, Father Donald Byrne reached the crest of the hill and immediately collapsed on the grass. He gulped huge mouthfuls of air, sucking it down into lungs red-raw and burning with the effort of extracting enough oxygen to meet the demands of muscles and limbs pushed to the limit of their endurance. He lay helplessly, stretched out face down in the crucifix position. A pulse thumped in his temple and echoed in his chest as his bloodstream circulated relentlessly and restored the badly depleted supplies of energy-giving oxygen. His breathing gradually subsided over a period of minutes to a more normal rate. He rolled over on to his back. His track suit hood blinkered him, framing an ellipse of sky and a group of dimly shining stars. Beyond the edges of the sight-limiting hood Byrne sensed the presence of people. There were always plenty of people about on Calton Hill at night, mostly innocent tourists and far-from-innocent homosexuals seeking their own kind to commit their particular brand of sin.

Below them, the city of Edinburgh spread out evenly, following the contours of the land in every direction to the River Forth in the north and the Pentland Hills in the south. The castle crowned the central rock alongside the arrow-straight avenue of Princes Street. The old Royal High School building was on one side and buildings proliferated everywhere at the foot of the hill like a growth of yeast. In the streets between, tiny people scurried for shelter.

At his feet was the incomplete Greek-style temple that would have been a memorial to the dead of the Napoleonic wars if the money had not run out before the job was finished. And above his head from where he lay, across a sea of roofs and graveyards and hidden streets, Salisbury Crags formed a dark wall guarding the hump of Arthur's Seat in the centre of Holyrood Park. It was easy for Byrne to appreciate why Greek civilisation placed the home of their omnipotent, vengeful gods on a mountain. All the better for throwing thunderbolts from.

He had dressed quickly while Lillian watched him from her nest of pillows on the bed, pulling on the vest and shorts and the light blue track suit with its bright yellow shoulder flashes. The bulky training shoes seemed too large for his narrow ankles. The sweat band round his head of short-cropped hair completed the image of the dedicated jogger. He had snapped smaller sweat bands on his wrists and retrieved the silver crucifix from the living-room floor to stuff it into a deep pocket for safe keeping.

'Same time next week,' Lillian said from the bedroom.

She was sitting upright against the pillows. The bed covers were bundled round her waist and she was buffing her fingernails with a cleaning pad. Her head was framed in a cloud of tousled hair and her nipples were like dark pink stains on the small mounds of her breasts.

He was a priest for God's sake, momentarily shocked at the shameless flaunting of her body. How had he let this happen? And it wasn't just the sex with Lillian, but everything else that had followed on from it.

'It's rude to stare,' Lillian had said, staring back at him in a way that seemed to penetrate through to his very soul.

Byrne had used to regard himself as a simple sinner. He used to think it had been his idea to take advantage of Lillian when she came to the church looking for solace as a confused young woman with no one to turn to. She had cried on his shoulder and he had comforted her. She had wept and he had kissed the tears away, but once the tears were all gone he did not stop kissing her.

Sin had been his excuse and his justification as he carried on his outward role of priest. He was a liar, a hypocrite, a deceiver, and a fraud. But these were human failings and one day, he felt sure, he would have the strength to overcome them and repent. It was a simple equation, making a mockery of the theological treatises he had been commended for in the seminary. It was too easy to claim that a spirit of evil had taken possession of him; to claim that it guided him and controlled him, forcing him to commit despicable acts; to claim that it, and not him, was responsible for the obscenity of his words and deeds; to claim that the real Donald Byrne could only cower inside the fragile shell of his physical body, a witness to all that happened in his name.

No, he was a sinner and the hardest part was the recognition that he gained an intense thrill from his depraved behaviour. The Church's theory of possession would explain it as being like whisky poured down someone's throat against their will. He became intoxicated by what happened and began to crave it more and more but it was hardly his fault.

19

Byrne believed more in free will. He alone was responsible for his actions, not some invisible, inaudible, intangible demon. He alone had decided to participate in a sexual relationship in direct contravention to morality and his priestly vows. There was no excuse. And afterwards, in quiet moments, he prayed for her soul.

He ran away from Lillian, out on to the streets, hiding in the shadows of the track suit hood. He ran himself to a standstill after leaving the flat, forcing his aching legs to run up the steep grassy side of Calton Hill at least twenty times, until he collapsed from exhaustion. He had run until his lungs and throat glowed red hot like an overheated engine, until the sweat ran freely all over his body and the very marrow of his bones began to hurt.

It was a small penance he demanded of himself, and a useless one. The truth was he enjoyed having sex with Lillian and everything that implied. He rather enjoyed being a sinner. Sex and corruption excited him and he would enjoy being a rich man when his plans eventually came to fruition. He had a half-formed, half-believed fantasy of setting up a children's orphanage somewhere in Eastern Europe. No one need know where the money came from. He would be regarded as a saint, a male Mother Theresa. He would strike a bargain, make his peace with God by helping starving children. He would be a shining example to others, so long as they did not know the truth.

Byrne stood up. His legs were weak, his knees stiff. A nagging pain swam round his head like a goldfish round a bowl. He began to jog down the slope towards a city swamped in darkness. Shreds of loathing and self-pity floated impotently in the whirlpool of emotions inside his mind. It was always like this after his weekly sex session. And he was already counting the days until the next.

7

The badly pot-holed farm track led up to an old farm steading that had been converted into a dwelling house. Gus Barrie, driving without lights, stopped the Transit van twenty yards from the wall and the indistinct shape of a parked car. The faces of the Jones brothers appeared beside his over the back of the seat, peering out through the windscreen. The moving sinews in Sandy's profiled neck made the lion tattoo growl silently.

'Is he there?' he asked.

'He's there,' Barrie replied.

'How can you be sure?'

'I'm sure. Watch this.'

Barrie took his mobile phone from the pocket of his sheepskin coat and held it against the steering wheel. It made soft beeping noises when he punched a number in. It rang for a long time before it was answered. In the house a light went on behind a window blind, spilling faintly round its edges. Billy Jones nodded enthusiastically. Sandy giggled.

'Can I speak to Mr Craig, please,' Barrie said.

'Who is it?'

'A friend of the family.'

There was a pause. Music played in the background. Barrie kept his eyes fixed on the thin-edged rectangle of light hanging in the dark mass of the house. The van rocked in a violent gust of wind.

'Who is this?' asked a different, more high-pitched voice.

'It's me, Georgie Boy,' Barrie said quietly, unable to resist a self-indulgent smile of satisfaction.

'Who? Gus? Is that you? What do you want?'

'I want to talk to you.'

'Why?'

'It's about my brother.'

Barrie's smile vanished with the words. He held up a key with his free hand and Billy took it. The brothers clambered over the front seat and out of the van. Each carried a length of razor wire with leather handles attached at both ends. This was to be another trademark killing. They walked ahead, one in front of the other, quickly lost in the darkness.

'About Mike?' Georgie Craig was saying. 'Mike's a dead man. What is there to talk about?'

'The cash. I think I know where it is.'

'Fuck me. Not that old fantasy. It went up in smoke all those years ago, Gus. Face it. The cash is ash.'

'Not any more, Georgie Boy. I have it. I'll show it to you, if you like.'

The line hummed for several seconds. 'Why?' Craig asked abruptly.

'I've got a proposition for you, Georgie. You won't be able to refuse once you hear the deal.'

'You and I don't do business together, Gus. Not any more. We don't like each other. Remember?'

Shadows moved across the outside of the rectangle of light. Somewhere in the distance a dog barked.

'I've mellowed with age.' Small droplets of moisture formed on the phone where Barrie's breath was condensing against it. 'And I've got this million and a half to find.'

'I thought you said you had it.'

'I will have. That's the business. I don't like you, Georgie Boy. I wouldn't want you to get the wrong idea. But I need you for this one.'

'Why do you need me?'

'I'll explain. I need to meet you.'

'Where?'

'Somewhere.'

'When?'

'As soon as you like. I tell you what. I'll send my people round to arrange it.'

'Why not arrange it now?'

'Okay, Georgie Boy. Whatever you want. I'll send them round now.'

'What the fuck...'

Barrie pushed in the aerial against the palm of his hand. He put the phone away in his pocket without once taking his eyes off the flickering outline of the window. No silhouettes danced across the blind. There was no sound. Nothing to suggest the bloody mayhem that was happening inside, the blades slicing through soft flesh. The blood. The death. Barrie sat patiently waiting in the rocking van and used his imagination.

Five minutes later the Jones brothers appeared suddenly in front of the van, materialising out of the darkness.

22

'That's it done, boss,' Billy said casually as they climbed noisily over the seat and into the back. 'No problems.'

'Georgie Boy wasn't too happy about it,' Sandy said, stifling a giggle. 'He got quite angry. Lost his head even.'

8

The winter morning was cold but the air was clear and pleasant, icily pure on the insides of David Fyfe's lungs. The coarse, dew-damp grass steamed on the hillside all around and sucked at his ankles as he waded through it along the narrow sheep track. A few faint pinpricks of stars were just visible on the pale underbelly of the darkly translucent sky still in the process of shifting from night into day.

Fyfe leaned on his waist-high walking stick and looked at his watch. His black labrador Jill sat at his side with her greying muzzle pushed under his hand. Number Five, the eighteen-month-old runt of Jill's only litter, was investigating interesting smells round some bushes one hundred yards distant, constantly looking back to check the two of them were still there.

In the house at the foot of the hill his ex-wife Sally was waiting for him to drive her the twenty miles into Edinburgh to catch the train at Waverley. More than a year had passed since the cause of Sally's illness. On occasions it seemed an eternity, at other times a mere blink of the eye. The picture of her lying prone under the madman's bleeding body was still fresh in Fyfe's mind. Standing on the hillside he could still feel the pressure of the narrow strip of metal on the soles of his feet where he had balanced on top of the railings to aim the gun through the window. It was another world, another life, viewed through the bullet hole in the shattered glass. He had thought Sally was dead but she had come back to life and then, incredibly, back to live with him. It was what he had thought he always wanted. But he had always wanted other things too.

Fyfe turned and began to retrace his steps along the dark green pathway he had made through the grass. Jill jumped up and barked at the suddenness of the movement. Number Five came scampering across at once, running straight into Fyfe's legs and almost knocking him over. He reached down and shook her roughly by the head while she playfully tried to bite his hands.

Sally had come through some pretty nasty bouts of depression. She would refuse to get out of bed, refuse to wash, refuse to dress, refuse to leave the house. At times she was suicidal. The worst thing for him was when she would cry for hours on end for no apparent reason. Great sobs would wrack her body, bubbles of misery rising from the very bottom of her soul, affecting him like hard punches to the guts. There was nothing he could do to comfort her. Nothing that did any good. He put his arms round her and squeezed her tight but could not share any of it. He could only watch and suffer vicariously. She had come through it herself and now she was about to leave on a journey south for a long-planned weekend at their daughter's home. She wanted to travel alone, leaving Fyfe on his own, just like it used to be.

The dogs raced on ahead down the hillside and through the gap in the hedge into the back garden. A bat whirred close to Fyfe's head and merged with the tangle of branches of the big sycamore tree by the kitchen door. He kicked off his walking boots and the waterproof leggings and went inside. The sound of the dogs' claws pattering on the vinyl floor was like bony fingers tapping impatiently on a window pane. The table had been cleared of breakfast debris. In the hallway Sally's suitcase was waiting behind the front door. The dogs were sitting beside it, flapping their tails, determined not to be left behind. Everything was ready for the departure.

Fyfe put on his normal shoes and his working jacket and raincoat. He loaded the cases into the boot and the dogs into the back seat. Watery sunshine was lightening the air. He went back into the house to get his briefcase. Sally was checking the locks on the windows in the living-room. Fyfe felt a slight tension creep into his bones. He had wanted her back, had always had the utmost confidence it would work out with them back together again. Now he had the vague, unformed impression that something was about to go very badly wrong. He couldn't ignore it because he trusted his senses the way a bloodhound trusts its nose. He had been uneasy for the last few weeks, unable to shake a morbid feeling that circumstances outwith his control were once more conspiring to shape his future no matter what he did. The feeling had started when the tenants did a moonlight flit from the Edinburgh New Town flat Sally had bought for refuge when they first separated. He could not explain it to anyone, least of all to Sally. It was paranoia pure and simple, like the conspiratorial voices he heard whispering outside his office.

Then Hunky Dunky the Chief Constable had phoned out of the blue to say there was a little job that needed doing. Fyfe sensed something major was about to happen but he had no idea what it might be. All he could do was wait to see what happened and take it from there. The story of his life so far.

'Don't worry about me. I'll be fine,' Sally said, coming over and holding his chin as a mother would a sulking child.

Fyfe hadn't realised he was staring into space. On the hillside with the dogs that morning he had looked up at the fast disappearing stars in the see-through sky and listened to the wind, hoping for some clue to what the future might hold. Nice view. No clue.

'I'll be fine too,' he replied. 'Even if you are abandoning me.'

They travelled up to Edinburgh in the kind of comfortable silence that can only be achieved by long-time lovers and friends. Every now and then Sally would remind him of what he had to do, what he should eat, not to use the dishwasher because the seal on the door was leaking. At Waverley Station he double-parked and carried her case on to the train. She settled down with a book and a pile of magazines and insisted he didn't need to wait. Impatient passengers shoved past him in the aisle. He kissed her and left. She waved at him from the window. He walked back to the car.

'We're on our own now, girls,' he said to the dogs. 'Do you think we can survive?'

9

The governor of Saughton Prison had grey toothbrush hair, teeth like fence-posts, and an unhealthy, colourless complexion. He sat behind a huge dark wood desk, fingering the base of an Anglepoise lamp as he studied the contents of a green cardboard folder. The desk top was scrupulously tidy. There was a blotting pad and a disproportionately large intricate glass and silver inkwell, its appearance spoiled by the cheap pens and pencils poking out of it. Three lead soldiers marching in different directions were fused together as a paperweight on top of another green cardboard folder. On one edge stacks of sheets of paper were stored in two black plastic three-tier trays. On the other edge was a combined telephone and intercom deck. In the centre was a name plate like a bar of Toblerone chocolate bearing the name J. J. Black.

Adamson stood with his hands clasped behind his back. He was wearing casual clothes, trousers and a jacket with just a hint of flamboyance in the bright red handkerchief in the breast pocket. He did not look at the governor but past him, over his shoulder at the plastic moulded lion and unicorn on either side of the coat of arms on the wall. Through the window he could see into the exercise yard. Adamson frowned as he waited to be spoken to. He had been excused the normal dog-box method of release where they shut you in a tiny windowless cubicle just to remind you who was boss while they checked your details. A dozen times he had followed the routine in his training-for-freedom days. The dog boxes, so cramped there was not enough space to turn round, always smelled of shoe polish and sweat and worse. All night he had been imagining himself in and out of them, then filling his lungs as he walked out into the fresh air beyond the wire. When they turned him right instead of left and took him upstairs at the administration block he was instantly suspicious, worried that it was some kind of trick. But it wasn't. He supposed it was some kind of honour. They couldn't do anything to him now. He had paid his debt, served his time.

Adamson had never been in the governor's office before. There seemed to be something strange about the window but he couldn't think what. Outside a remote control camera mounted on a corner swung lazily to and fro surveying the emptiness. Of course, he suddenly realised with a tremor of a smile. No bars.

'John Adamson,' the governor said, nodding his head sagely as if he was coming out with some profound comment.

Adamson nodded back. 'That's right, Mr Black. Sir. John Adamson.'

The governor looked up, still nodding, sucking in his top lip. Adamson tried not to smile but felt his mouth twitching involuntarily. Black was relatively new, in charge at Saughton for less than a year. Adamson had never spoken to him and wasn't particularly interested in speaking to him now. Self-confidence swelled inside Adamson but he didn't want to take any chances till he was safely out through the gates. He could play the game to their rules for a few minutes more. His release was already two hours overdue. He wasn't going to complain. He could wait.

'Armed robbery,' Black said. 'A serious crime, armed robbery.'

'It won't be happening again, sir.'

'No?' Black raised his eyebrows and his whole face seemed to flatten out. 'I certainly hope not. You've been turned down by the parole board a few times before now.'

'It won't happen again.'

His record showed that one million pounds plus had never been recovered after the robbery. Five times the parole board had asked him if he knew where it was. Five times he replied that if it had not been burned to a crisp as he believed then it had gone to Spain and was probably long spent. Four times they took exception to his attitude and refused him parole. The fifth time he repeated the same story about being a youngster drawn into crime against his better judgement. He was more mature now, more responsible, more independent. He had learned his lesson but, no, he didn't know where the money was. The four-person panel, two elderly men in smart suits and two younger women who smelled of static electricity and deodorant, looked at each other and wrote things down. They either believed him, or had finally given up trying to wear him down. The recommendation was for early release. He was on his way out.

'You're not a bad lad, Adamson. My officers speak well of you.'

'Thank you, sir.'

'You've performed well here. You've co-operated. You've made it easy on yourself.'

'Thank you, sir.'

28

'You've been a model prisoner.'

'Thank you, sir.'

Adamson decided to stop himself saying thank you in case it was taken for sarcasm. Black continued to talk, producing all the old clichés about crime not paying and honesty being the best policy in the end. A civilised society had to have rules otherwise it degenerated into anarchy. The rules had to be in place to allow society to survive. There was no tenable moral debate about it. There was good and there was bad and the good had the right to control the bad in the interests of the majority.

'Rules are not made to be broken,' Black said. 'Don't let anybody ever tell you that. Rules are made to be respected.'

Adamson almost said 'Thank you, sir' but stopped himself, destroying the partly formed words by clearing his throat. He raised his hand to his mouth and watched the governor's eyes. They were so pale they blended with the whiteness of his skin. His lips were bloodless too. Even his suit was a dull grey, and his shirt, and his tie. Only his earlobes had any colour about them, a distinct pinkish tinge. The sky behind Black, a patch of it seen through the unbarred window, was a beautifully clear blue. I can wait, Adamson thought. I can wait.

The governor sat back and the sudden movement made pages inside the folder spill out, spoiling the symmetry of the desk top. He sat forward again to straighten them up and then eased himself back more carefully.

'You're lucky, Adamson,' Black said. 'You're going out to a flat, a job, and the proper guidance of people who care about you. Not many leave here with those advantages. Don't ruin it for yourself. Stay on the straight and narrow. Obey the rules.'

'Yes, sir. I am lucky, sir. I know that.'

'That's all I have to say.'

Black leaned forward. He lifted the trio of fused lead soldiers and put the green folder on top of the other one underneath it. Then he reached for the intercom and held down a switch.

'Mr Stewart, you can send in…' Black rubbed a finger across his mouth, trying to remember the name. 'You can send in…er…send in Adamson's sponsor.'

'Thank you, sir,' Adamson said, grinning openly as he fought a strong urge to spit in Black's face.

He turned away from the desk, moving slowly and deliberately to emphasise the fact that he was not asking for permission. The waiting was over at last. The door opened and Adamson's smile grew even wider at the sight of the person who had come to take him away from the prison.

'Am I glad to see you,' he said.

Father Donald Byrne entered the room. Black looked on approvingly as he shook hands and embraced Adamson in a gentle bear hug.

'Jad, my boy,' the priest said. 'Didn't I promise your mother I'd look after you?'

10

Fyfe had time to let Jill and Number Five out for a run at Granton, down by the shore on the grass at Gypsy Brae, before he went in to the Fettes headquarters. He didn't want to be too early, to be seen to jump when Hunky Dunky whistled. He hoped the little job would involve getting out of the office so he did not have to leave the dogs cooped up in the car. If he was really stuck he could dump them on Sally's cousin Catriona at her house just along the road in Craigleith.

He checked with the Chief Constable's secretary when he got in then made himself some coffee and hid away to read the daily papers. One of the civilian secretaries knocked on the half-open door and entered. It was young Mary. He couldn't remember her second name. She was young and friendly but not particularly good at the job she had been doing for only three weeks. Fyfe didn't care about her efficiency because she was a delight to look at, all bouncing curves, shining eyes, and a jumble of gold chains at a smooth white throat. At least her heart is in the right place, he thought, surreptitiously glancing at the place where her heart was.

'I typed out these reports for the fiscal last night, Chief Inspector,' she said brightly.

Fyfe sighed. The hem of Mary's short skirt was several inches above the level of his desk. Her blouse was semi-see-through and her bra was lace-trimmed. The sun was shining outside without producing any heat. Stormy weather was reported to be moving down the coast from the north.

'Nice job, Mary,' he said, skimming through the pages without really looking. 'You can be my secretary and sit on my knee any time.'

'Chance would be a fine thing.'

'Our relationship would be strictly professional.'

'Strictly. As strict as you like. How about some coffee?'

He had just finished one mug and didn't want any more, but he didn't want to refuse either. He could easily imagine himself and Mary in a compromising position. One of his problems had always been that he liked women too much. He liked Mary because she knew nothing about his troubled history in the force, the brush with alcoholism, the pop-eyed psychologist messing with his brain to put him right. She only knew that he was a kind of folk hero because he had shot to kill when required. They couldn't sack heroes, only sideline them to keep them out of the way.

'No, thanks,' he said.

'Another time then.'

Detective Sergeant Bill Matthewson collided with Mary in the doorway and stood back deferentially to allow her out. He came in looking backwards to watch her walking between the desks in the squad room. Her generous buttocks swung from side to side and not a man she passed in the operations room failed to admire them.

'The tourist board should declare this a site of great scenic beauty,' Fyfe said. 'We could charge people to come and look at the view.'

'Name your price,' Matthewson said, still looking backwards.

Matthewson was under thirty but had old man's bags under his eyes and looked a lot older than Fyfe. He had a well-proportioned body but somehow his face was all wrong. The ears and mouth were too big, eyes too close together, nose squint, and chin too square. He was a Highlander, originally from the far north-west, and talked with a musical singsong lilt.

'Was there something you wanted, Sergeant?' Fyfe asked. 'Apart from young Mary, that is.'

'Uh. Yes, sir. Sir Duncan wants to talk to you.'

'Yes, I know. Promotion or demotion? Which do you think?'

Matthewson shrugged and left the office. Fyfe followed him and walked to the lift. On the short two-floor journey he began day-dreaming about slapping a resignation letter down in front of Hunky Dunky before he got a chance to explain what his little job was about. All Fyfe lacked was the letter. He might try it verbally but he would probably be regarded as drunk. Face it, he thought contemptuously, you're not going to do or say anything. You'll run any errand that is asked of you.

Fyfe disliked Sir Duncan intensely because the pompous bastard was so condescending. He should have sacked him all those years ago when he was a newly promoted inspector, a faithless husband, under investigation for beating up suspects and drunk and incapable in the squad room late at night. He could have sacked him and he should have but he didn't, thereby emphasising his moral superiority and his exclusive access to the prerogative of mercy. Fyfe was tucked nicely into his pocket for future patronisation. He wasn't even demoted, just lectured on the evils of drink, patted on the back and shoved in front of the cure-all shrink.

Fyfe should have resigned, but he didn't. At the time he was just glad to keep his job. He never expected to be promoted but once he was briefly famous after the shooting incident they had no choice but to grudgingly make him up to chief. Then he was put out of harm's way as third in command of the Fraud Squad.

Sir Duncan's secretary looked up from her word processor, nodded and waved him into the office. Sir Duncan was not in uniform. He was seated on a chair by the window, elbows balanced on his knees as he packed tobacco into his pipe. The watery daylight through the window endowed his generous mop of grey hair with an unusual metallic sheen.

'David,' he said. 'Come in. Come in. Good to see you. We'll have to make this quick, I'm afraid. I've got to go and meet with our esteemed council leaders to try and persuade them to fix next year's budget at a level that won't mean riots on the streets. Sit down. Sit down.'

Fyfe watched Sir Duncan light his pipe. It took three matches. The tiny blip of flame fattened as it was sucked into the bowl and contracted as it emerged again. Each match burned right down to the end before being snuffed out.

'That's it,' Sir Duncan said, satisfied that the tobacco was smouldering efficiently. 'Now, David, I want to ask you a personal favour. Something we can keep between ourselves.'

This was the little job. Short of a request to kill the first-born of the city, there was no way Fyfe could refuse. 'Ask away, sir,' he said.

'Archbishop John Delaney is a good friend of mine. He and I are on a number of committees together. I was talking to him the other day. He was looking for some advice.'

'Yes, sir.'

'Are you a Catholic, David?'

'No, sir.'

'Church of Scotland?'

'Not really.'

'A Wee Free then?'

'No, sir. I'm an agnostic.'

'Good for you. Shows an independence of mind and spirit. I'm a Protestant myself. United Free. I've been baptised so I get to go to heaven and I go to church every week to hear the latest news on the damned.

Imagine me advising an Archbishop. Funny the way things happen, isn't it? I don't know if my minister would approve.'

'Yes, sir.'

Fyfe guessed what was coming next. Somebody nicking the collection money or drinking the communion wine. Just about the level of serious crime Hunky Dunky would consider him competent enough to be entrusted with.

'John has a slight problem,' Sir Duncan said and the stem of his pipe clicked against teeth. 'I'd like you to go and see him. He is expecting you. It appears somebody has been fiddling the Church accounts. Nothing too substantial but it would be embarrassing for the Church if it was to become public knowledge.'

'You want me to find out who is doing it?'

'Yes. John already has a prime suspect. He wants a confession and he thinks a real policeman might be enough to get it.'

'Is it a priest?'

'Apparently so. Temptation must have been too much for him.'

'I would have thought he answered to a higher authority than Her Majesty's police.'

'Only once he leaves our jurisdiction. David, I'd be grateful if you'd play along with the Archbishop. I need John's support on a number of other issues.' He tapped his pipe meaningfully on an empty ashtray. 'Politics, you understand. Back scratching. That kind of thing.'

'Of course, sir.'

'I doubt if there will be charges involved. The Procurator Fiscal doesn't know about it and I'd like to keep it that way if possible. A real live detective on the case is what John wants. He thinks that will put a seal on it, convince his errant priest to come clean.'

'I'm flattered.'

'I have to go,' Sir Duncan said distractedly. He stood up and Fyfe copied him. 'I'm sure I can trust you with this one, David. It's a bit out of the ordinary but I'm sure you'll be able to sort it out quietly. John is expecting you to see him this morning. There isn't anyone else I could ask to do this. I've taken to regarding you as my troubleshooter.'

'Thank you, sir.'

Fyfe left and called the lift in the corridor. He liked the idea of the job. Plenty of play-acting and no paperwork. If he was lucky he could justify running it into a few days of next week, maybe the whole week. Troubleshooter, eh? He liked the sound of that even if it was a bit of a back-handed compliment to say that there was nobody else on the force capable of handling it. Should he be flattered to be picked out or did it mean no one else could be spared from real police work?

Downstairs he called Matthewson into his office. 'Handing over to you meantime, Bill. I've been redeployed on a secret mission.'

'Really? Not the murder, is it?'

'What murder?'

'Body on the beach at Portobello. Throat cut.'

'Drugs, is it? Anybody important?'

'Don't think so. Don't know the story yet. They think there could be another body around. Anonymous call came in this morning telling us about the body at Porty and another one, location unknown.'

'He's not mine. I can't discuss my case, naturally, but it doesn't yet have dead bodies associated with it. The good news is that hopefully it has nothing to do with VAT frauds or tax scams, or crooked lawyers nicking old ladies' life savings. It is real crime. It has a touch of malice, a hint of violence, a pinch of sheer badness. A bit like a body on the beach with its throat cut.'

'Yes, sir.'

'There are plenty of bad people out there. All we have to do is catch a couple of them every now and again and the public feel safe sleeping in their beds. That's why I joined the police, you know; to catch the bad guys.'

'You've caught a few in your time,' Matthewson said.

'What?'

'I said you've caught a few in your time,' Matthewson repeated reluctantly, embarrassed by the sentence when he heard it the second time around. 'Well, you have.'

'Don't be patronising, Sergeant.'

'Sorry, sir.'

'Actually, I never really wanted to be a detective, you know, Bill.'

'You didn't, sir?'

'No. I wanted to be a lumberjack.'

'Really, sir?'

'No. I'm lying. A good policeman has to be able to suss out when people are lying or taking the piss. It makes the job a lot easier. I like to think experience contributes a lot to the way you regard people. There's no substitute for it.'

Matthewson's face had turned pink. 'Yes, sir. I'll work at it.'

'Now I have to go visit an Archbishop. Maybe he's going to confess to something juicy.'

'Stranger things have happened.'

'Not this week. Not so far anyway.'

Matthewson left the room with the reports under his arm. Fyfe saw him flap his hand up and down in front of his face, pantomiming burned fingers to colleagues at their desks. Fyfe was disappointed that he had resorted to sarcasm to put Matthewson down. He used to have a decent rapport with other people but that seemed to have vanished. All he did now was put their backs up and antagonise them for no good reason. Maybe a blow-out to ease the pressure would help. Not a full-scale binge like in the old days but just a good night's drinking. It might make him more bearable, more human. He was reasonably certain that, if he asked, young Mary would obligingly sit in his lap. What could be more human than that?

Meanwhile there was the Archbishop to attend to. Fyfe looked up his number in the phone book. A mature woman answered and there was a brief silence when he unthinkingly addressed her as Mrs Delaney, slapping himself theatrically on the forehead when he realised what he had done.

'I'm sorry,' he said contritely. 'You won't be... You can't be...'

'I'm not,' the voice announced primly. 'I am the Archbishop's housekeeper. You will find him at the diocesan office.'

That was in the book under Catholic Church. Fyfe dialled and talked to a woman who sounded like the twin sister of the housekeeper. She had been expecting to hear from him and told him to come round straight away. Fyfe was getting up to go when his phone rang. He sat down again to answer it.

'DCI Fyfe here. Can I help you?'

'David. It's me.'

He recognised the voice immediately. Surprise made him sit up straight. It must have been over a year since he had last heard it but the familiarity suggested days, hours even, rather than long months. He pictured the lips forming the words that were being spoken into his ear, the line of her nose, the way her hair fell over her eyes. Fyfe cupped the receiver behind the palm of his hand.

'Sylvia,' he said. 'It's good to hear from you. How have you been?'

'About average. And you?'

'Not too bad.'

'Long time no see. Have you been avoiding me?'

'Not by choice,' he protested. 'Certainly not.'

There was no animosity between his former lover Sylvia Cranston, the high-flying advocate, and his ex-wife Sally. Never had been. He had assumed his affair with her was over when Sally had moved back to live with him. Anyway, he had never lived with Sylvia for more than one night at a time. She had visited his home in the Borders once while Sally was ill. It was Sylvia's way of showing that she was no longer a rival. When she left she kissed him on the cheek and squeezed his hand. Thanks for having me. See you around, old friend.

He had seen her only a few times since then, always by chance, usually around the courts, but he had never completely blocked her out of his mind. She was always present, had been there last night and in the morning on the hillside when he was staring up into the sky. The flesh on the back of his neck prickled. She was a part of his life. He loved Sylvia dearly but would never be able to tell her so.

'I'm phoning to invite you to a party.'

'Good. I haven't been to a party for ages.' And Sally's away for the weekend too, he thought automatically.

'It's my engagement party.'

'Your engagement party?' He tried to sound indifferent but his voice definitely rose in pitch. There was a sharp element of jealousy in his surprise. 'I didn't know you were engaged.'

'Well, I am, and it is a cause for great celebration.'

'Who is the lucky man?'

'My father.'

'I beg your pardon?'

'Yes. You know how incestuous the legal profession is. I'm going to marry my father.'

'Do I laugh at the joke now?'

'My Devilmaster. The man who trained me before I became an advocate. I call him my father. It's a legal term we use to confuse outsiders.'

'Okay, I'm confused. So who is your father?'

'Graeme Hughes, aka Lord Greenmantle.'

'The High Court judge?'

'That's him.'

'You're going to marry Lord Greenmantle?'

'Guilty as charged.'

Fyfe wanted to say that Lord Greenmantle was old enough to be her father, that she couldn't possibly be serious, that she was far too young and good-looking to throw herself away on a dried-up old fart, that she must have taken leave of her senses, that she was doing it on the rebound from him, that it was ridiculous. But then what right had he to be jealous or to tell Sylvia what to do? A spasm of anger made him clench his free fist. The coffee cup cracked and the lukewarm brown liquid spilled over his fingers.

'Congratulations,' he said. 'You little devil you.'

'Thanks very much,' she replied. 'You will come, won't you?'

'When is it?'

'Tomorrow. Say you'll come. I know it's short notice but there will be an awful lot of boring people there. I need to see a friendly face.'

'I would like to but it's rather short notice,' Fyfe said, seizing the let out she had given him. 'What brought this invitation on, Sylvia? Am I an afterthought?'

'Never, Dave. I just suddenly thought how nice it would be to see you again.'

'It would be, wouldn't it?'

'Well, I hope you can make it, Dave. Just knock on the door and say the password.'

'What's that?'

'My name.'

'What's your name again?'

'Think about it. It'll come back to you. I'll maybe see you then?'

'Maybe. But let's keep in touch anyway, even if you are going to be a married woman.'

'You used to be a married man when we were in touch before.'

'What are we now?' Fyfe asked.

'Just good friends.'

'See you then.'

'Yes. See you.'

Fyfe replaced the receiver and sat back in his chair, turning to look out the window, drying his hand with a piece of scrap paper and mopping up the mess of coffee on the desk. He was on his own. That meant he could go to Sylvia's party and Sally would never know. What she didn't know couldn't hurt her. It was the first time Sally had been away from home since they had got back together again. Strange how the invitation should come just as he found himself in a position to accept it. He wanted to go, wanted to see Sylvia face to face and find out what she was playing at. Circumstances were conspiring to permit him to do just that.

Fyfe narrowed his eyes and a stand of out-of-focus trees in the near distance waved in a sudden explosive downdraught of wind. The bare branches splayed out and sprang back into shape.

He was definitely uneasy. Things were happening out there, he thought. Things had already happened. Soon all those things would combine in a pattern that would make sense. The real trick would be to make sense of it while the pattern was still taking shape. No chance of that.

11

The car nosed carefully round the rain-filled holes of the car-park and manoeuvred into an empty space. The engine spluttered a couple of times after the ignition was turned off and finally died with a sudden cough.

'Your timing's off,' Adamson said.

'Yes. She needs tuning,' Byrne replied. 'I know a mechanic who will do it but he hasn't been to confession for a while. Now, if you'll just wait a moment I'll have this collar off and I'll treat you to a drink in your first hour of freedom.'

'Why take off the collar?'

'It upsets some people to see a priest doing the normal things that normal people do, like going into a pub for a drink. For some reason it makes them feel guilty and there's enough guilt in this world without me adding to it needlessly. So I'll go incognito. There. I could pass for a real person now, couldn't I? Don't I look normal.'

'Definitely, Father.'

'And not so much of the Father. I'm hardly old enough to be your big brother. Call me Donald if you will.'

'Okay, Donald.'

They got out of the car and walked together to the pub door. Inside the place was hung with horse brasses and hunting pictures. There were two men on high stools and two women at a corner table, one wearing a hat. The unsmiling barmaid, a young girl with dirty blonde hair, a painted face and tight T-shirt, unfolded her arms as they entered and leaned on her hands on the bar, arching her eyebrows by way of silent inquiry.

'What will you have then, Jad?' Byrne asked.

Adamson had avoided pubs on his training-for-freedom days and weekends. The only alcohol that he had drunk in nine years had been the occasional cupful of highly acidic home brew produced in a forgotten corner of a prison store from rotting pears and oranges and sold at fifty pence a go by an enterprising inmate doing time for tax fraud. It caused terrible stomach cramps, scoured your brain like a Brillo pad, but each new bucketful sold within hours. Once a week he allowed himself to smoke some expensively obtained cannabis as a relaxant and a reward for getting closer to getting out. Otherwise, the sight and the smell of the junkies who jagged themselves with all sorts of inventive solutions and powders were more than enough to deter him from following that path. He preferred to watch old black and white films. Hitchcock was his hero and the flickering celluloid a strong drug that ate up the hours of enforced idleness. All thoughts of women were consigned to a mental backwater in his brain from where they emerged at irregular intervals, despite the nightly films, the weekly dope, and the occasional alcohol, to frustrate him intensely.

But now he was free and out on his own. There were no limiting factors any more, no restraints. He could drink as much as he liked and have as many women as he liked. He realised he was staring at the barmaid's substantial breasts pushing against the stretched yellow material of the T-shirt and jerked his eyes away to the well-stocked gantry and its rows of spirit bottles. Freedom made him feel dizzy.

The barmaid turned, displaying a backside stacked up by jeans tighter than her T-shirt. In that instant, all his fears for the future fell away and the idea that he had once coveted the three-meals-a-day and warm-bed-at-night security of prison life shrivelled like a piece of burning paper. As soon as he dumped the guilt-inducing Father Donald he would start to enjoy himself properly.

He accepted a pint and declined the offer of something to eat. Byrne took a gin and tonic and they found a table to sit facing each other. Adamson was embarrassed, not knowing what to say. His mother had been the holy one, going to Mass every day and keeping little plaster saints on window ledges all over the house. Adamson had never known Byrne. He had come into the picture only after her death, claiming in prison visits that she had made him vow to look after her only son. He had not harassed Adamson, had not demanded he attend church services or study the scriptures or anything like that. He had simply visited him a couple of times for casual, time-killing chats. And he had organised a flat normally devoted to his parish's drug rehabilitation programme, and a coming-out job stocking shelves in a supermarket.

Adamson should have been grateful for his time and trouble, but there was something about the man he was not sure of, something about his manner and his attitude. Byrne acted like a prison officer whose assumption that he controlled all aspects of your life was instinctive and unthinking. That was the priest in him. It would be good, Adamson thought, sipping his cold beer, to get away from him at the earliest opportunity.

'Your mother would have been a happy woman this day,' Byrne said.

Adamson nodded and looked around. He was always reluctant to talk about his mother.

'She was a proud woman. Proud of her son, she was. I remember her telling me how much she was looking forward to you being released and going back to live with her. "He'll take good care of me, will my son," she said. "I won't have anything to worry about when he gets back. No money worries ever again."'

Adamson twitched at the mention of money. He glanced across the table to see Byrne staring straight at him and looked away hurriedly. But he could not keep his gaze averted. His head slowly turned back again as if an invisible hand was guiding his chin. It moved round until the eyes of the two men locked together.

He thinks he knows about the cash, Adamson thought. She must have told him my secret. A sense of desperate amusement made Adamson bite the inside of his lip. Jesus Christ, he thinks he knows.

'It is a tremendous thing, the love of a mother for her son,' Byrne was saying, the pattern of his speech falling into hypnotic rhythm. 'One of God's most precious gifts on this earth. It is the closest bond between two people that can exist. A mother and her son should have no secrets. Wouldn't you agree, Jad? The bond between a mother and her son?'

Adamson felt disorientated. He lifted his pint glass but did not attempt to drink any of it.

'Your mother is dead now, may God have mercy on her soul, but before she died she asked me to take on the responsibility for you, Jad. I agreed. I hope I can take her place in your life, Jad. It may not be a mother's love I have to offer but it is a genuine form of love. If I am to help you, Jad, we should have no secrets from each other. No secrets at all.'

'No secrets.' Adamson shook his head. 'What do you want me to tell you?'

'I don't want you to tell me anything, Jad.' He patted the back of Adamson's hand where it lay on the table. 'I just want you to be able to trust me. That is what your mother would have wanted.'

The barmaid passed by collecting empty glasses. Adamson was disconcerted by the leer he detected in the priest's sideways glance. Something was wrong here. Badly wrong.

'Now, now, Jad,' Byrne said. 'I think a few thousand Hail Marys are in order to compensate for the impure thoughts you are harbouring about that young lady.'

Adamson's mouth fell open in amazement that a priest should make such a comment. He shifted nervously in his seat. Byrne chuckled and finger-stirred the ice cubes in his gin.

'Don't be shocked, Jad. I wasn't born a priest. I grew up to become one and before I took my vows I knew all about the urges young men like yourself are prone to. You more than most at the moment, having been locked up for the last nine years. I'm not embarrassing you, am I?'

'A little bit.'

'You'll get used to me.' Byrne leaned forward to speak more quietly. 'I tend to say what I think and what I'm thinking right now is that given half a chance you would have the knickers off that young lady and her arse spread-eagled over the bar there.'

Adamson choked on a mouthful of beer. Byrne leaned still closer and dropped his voice to a whisper. 'The things I hear, Jad. The secrets people tell me. Priests are party to knowledge of the weirdest desires and vices. The depths to which human beings can sink. The sins that are committed. We know it all.'

There was a bad taste in Adamson's mouth. Anxiety made his hands tremble and he clumsily folded his arms. He became super-sensitive to the thumping of his heartbeat and the flow of blood circulating round his body. Byrne had him frozen in his vision, like a rabbit in the glaring headlights of an approaching car. He thinks he knows, Adamson thought, and a mild tremor of laughter made him fidget. He thinks he knows.

'Do you trust me, Jad?'

'Of course I trust you, Donald,' Adamson lied.

'Do you? Do you really? Would you tell me your most precious secret?'

Adamson felt himself shrinking under the intensity of Byrne's stare. He had told his mother about the fabulous hidden fortune because he had wanted to put her mind at rest about how he would survive once she was dead. She must have told Byrne in the sanctity of the confessional. He might be a lapsed Catholic but he was well aware that no genuine priest would ever break that sanctity. It was a mortal sin. Wasn't that the way it was supposed to work? But then was Father Byrne a genuine priest? Who was he? What was he? What did Byrne want from him?

'I know about the money, Jad,' Byrne said.

Adamson seemed to be floating in the air with no sensation of any part of his body touching anything solid. Another tremor of laughter rose through his body like hiccups but he managed to resist it. He wished himself back inside the familiar little prison cell where no one could get at him. The interior of the pub began to compress around him. He wanted to get up and walk away but could not move.

'I know what you're thinking, Jad,' Byrne said softly. His nostrils widened when he smiled. He looked like somebody posing for his picture to be taken. He looked incredibly pleased with himself. A cat about to get the cream. 'Don't worry, Jad. I want to help you. The money is yours. You've served your time for it. I just want to keep my promise to your mother, that's all. I want to make sure you're all right. I'm not going to hand you over to the police or anything like that. Besides, you can't be punished twice for the same crime.'

'You're right, Donald,' Adamson said, suppressing the anxiety and enjoying a delicious wave of calmness. 'Why don't we go and get the money?'

It was Byrne's turn to be surprised. 'When?' he asked eagerly.

'No time like the present.' He held out his empty glass. 'First I'll have another drink. I'm beginning to get the taste for it.'

12

The gatehouse was hidden behind a high wall and a stand of poplar trees at the entrance to the half-mile long driveway to Gus Barrie's home. In Victorian times it had been the estate gamekeeper's house but no one had actually lived in it for more than fifty years. The stonework was in poor condition and slates were missing from the roof. The wooden beams forming the eaves were badly eroded. Every window was sealed with an ancient plywood panel and a more recently installed black-painted grid of closely spaced iron bars. The padlocks linking the grids to metal tabs cemented into the walls were still bright and shiny. The arched doorway had a similar grid and padlock arrangement on hinges.

Barrie walked briskly down the drive, swinging a bunch of keys on a finger. He hadn't slept at all but he wasn't tired. The excitement of anticipation was making his heart race alarmingly fast. His mind was hyperactive. All night he had prowled the house, cocooned in the bubble of light created by the fancy electronic circuitry, the music trailing behind him. He refused to take any sleeping pills because he hated the idea of drugs contaminating his body. He still had a muscular frame, not an ounce of spare flesh on him. Every nerve bristled with energy and vigour. He was proud of his body. He had taken great care of it. He wanted Angie to be proud of it too.

His beloved Angie would soon be on her way to him and he had ensured that everything was prepared, everything perfect down to the last detail. The decks were cleared. Ross Sorley and Georgie Boy were among the last pieces of untidiness to be swept under the carpet. Now his house and his life were in order. The final detail would be slotted into place in front of Angie's beautiful eyes. Until that was over he could not relax. He had an obsessive need to check the gatehouse. Every day for the last week he had done it at least once, sometimes three times morning, afternoon and night.

Barrie opened two padlocks to free the exterior iron grid. A big old-fashioned key and two smaller ones at top and bottom opened the house's original iron bolt-studded door.

Barrie entered and locked the door shut behind him. Inside it was dark and very cold. He felt his way along the corridor and turned into the first room on the left, groping for the light switch and flicking it on. The single bare bulb hanging from the ceiling was hardly enough to dispel the gloom. Dust particles drifted lazily in the murky air. It was like being underwater. The room was empty apart from a large steel chest against one wall. Another much larger padlock secured it. Barrie looked up at the sound of scraping above his head. It came from the pigeons nesting in the attic space, disturbed by his presence.

Barrie knelt down beside the steel chest and inserted a key in the padlock. It clicked loudly and fell to the floor with a thud. He raised the lid as he stood up and smiled coldly. There were three bulging black sacks. One was open at the top. Ten-pound notes spilled from it like foam over the rim of a beer glass. Barrie spoke softly to himself, smiling at the image of himself as an old miser crouched over his hoard rubbing his hands with glee. But it wasn't his money. It belonged to someone else. Barrie's pleasure would be in handing it back to its rightful owner.

'One million, three hundred and seventy-five thousand, two hundred and forty-eight pounds,' he said. 'The bank's officially recorded loss. And it's all yours, Angela darling. Your inheritance.'

13

The freckle-faced, red-haired girl behind the reception desk of the diocesan office ticked off Fyfe's name on a list and signalled for him to have a seat while she phoned upstairs to inform the Archbishop. She pointed at the ceiling as she punched the extension number and reported his arrival.

'Someone will be down to collect you in a moment,' she said.

Fyfe sat cross-legged with his coat across his knees. A stream of warm air from a wall-mounted radiator made him glad he had dropped the dogs off at Catriona's on his way rather than have to leave them in the cold car any longer. The sun sparkled on the glass of the windows without adding to the heat.

The low table in front of Fyfe was covered with newspapers and religious magazines. Fie picked up the *Catholic Observer* and flicked through it without taking much notice of the contents until he came to a photograph of Archbishop Delaney on one of the pages shaking hands with a self-conscious nun. He had a fat, heavy-jowled face. His small eyes were deep-set and Fyfe thought he had a strange monk-style haircut before realising it was a skullcap and not a bald patch.

A sudden feeling of hostility, like a bad smell, affected him as he looked at the photograph. It wasn't religious prejudice, just that he had never felt comfortable around people like Catholic Bishops and Protestant ministers who claimed to have all the answers and would share them with anyone who pledged allegiance. It was a view shaped by his reluctant attendance as a young child at Sunday school in the local church, split up into small groups and dispersed widely among the creaking wooden pews so they could not distract each other. Sweet-smelling, teenage Miss Saunders guarded the only way in and out of the pew and when she read from the bible she always placed one hand gently on her hat as if she expected it to be blown away at any second. The clothes she wore crackled with starch and when she sat down she had a habit of wiggling her bum and pulling at the hem of her skirt while the boys stared at her legs. The bible stories were always boring and the hymn-singing off key. The moon-faced minister used to get dreadfully angry when no one volunteered answers to his questions. Fyfe had never admitted knowing any answer and rebellion went further when he and the other boys secretly carved symbols on to the underside of the polished wood with the edge of a threepenny bit. Nothing that would identify them, of course, just random scratchings, obscenities and hieroglyphics, pagan symbols to show the Church that here were tiny souls slipping through its grasping fingers.

Fyfe had discovered a problem with all authority figures from an early age. Elders and betters, he was told, and the finality of that statement created the strong suspicion that while the first description might be accurate, there was no guarantee the second one was. He worked out for himself that respect should be earned, not simply expected, in the adult world. That was how he judged his teachers and all the others he came into contact with.

The police constable who failed him the first time around in his cycling proficiency test but then took the trouble to explain exactly where he had gone wrong would never know how much influence he had on Fyfe's decision to join the force years later. It had been a strange experience for Fyfe, transforming himself into an authority figure. He liked to think he should have been a terrorist, a resistance fighter, a maverick politician, a lonely long distance runner, or one of those guys who rowed the Atlantic in an open boat. He should have been the archetypal loner looking from the edge of society in towards the centre. He fancied himself as a brooding pool of still water running deep, but the trouble with that was that he didn't really enjoy being alone at all. He needed to have people around him.

'Mr Fyfe?'

He looked up, frowning, annoyed to be woken from his pleasant daydream. He had forgotten where he was and the sun was hot on the back of his neck. He reached round with his hand and touched the warm flesh there, as warm as newly baked scones fresh from the oven, feeling it radiate into his palm. In front of him stood a small woman of maybe sixty with eyes hugely magnified by the thick lenses of her glasses to be out of all proportion to the rest of her face. The black pupils gaped at him like those he had seen so often on spaced-out drug addicts.

'Chief Inspector Fyfe?' she repeated in a scratchy voice. 'I'm Miss Lyle, Archbishop Delaney's personal secretary. The Archbishop will see you now.'

'Of course.'

He followed her across the foyer to the lift and they had to wait for it to arrive. She was wearing a black skirt and stiff white shirt buttoned up to the neck. She made some comment about the weather and he muttered a noncommittal reply. The red-haired receptionist smiled at him as he looked around, fighting the urge to whistle.

'Lovely day, isn't it?' Miss Lyle said loudly.

'Beautiful.'

'We should thank God.'

Does that mean we should blame him when it rains, Fyfe thought more cheerfully, applying the frustrating theological argument that had made his old Sunday school teacher blush because she could never answer it properly. The lift doors opened with a sharp ping and Fyfe went in after the woman, standing well away from her in the confined space so as not to seem threatening.

'It's a terrible thing,' she said when the doors scraped shut and the lift began to rise.

'What is?'

'When somebody steals money from the Church.'

Fyfe was taken aback. The secrecy conveyed by Sir Duncan had made him assume the Archbishop's suspicions were privileged information. Just how personal was this personal secretary if she shared such a sensitive secret? She had introduced herself as Miss Lyle. A spinster then, he thought negatively. A female version of the Archbishop without the fancy dress and shepherd's crook, finding solace only in her faith as she steadily got older. No children of her own, no grandchildren, just the Church and its childlike priests to fuss over.

Miss Lyle looked back at him over her shoulder. The glasses flashed under the lights as she turned her head. 'Don't be so surprised,' she said. 'I've worked here for more than thirty years and have seen four Archbishops laid in their graves. This is my fifth. He's not bad but definitely a bit of a ditherer. Archbishop Michaelson would have stopped it by now. He wouldn't have bothered with all this investigation business. He would just have stopped it.'

Fyfe felt compelled to say something. 'I'm not here officially. I have just come to listen and offer advice.'

'That's right, son. We don't want a scandal.' She gulped breaths between sentences. 'Just remember that Our Lady sees everything. Nothing can be hidden from her.'

One huge eye closed in a dramatic slow-motion wink. For a moment Fyfe saw her as she must have been when she was a younger woman, smooth-skinned and attractive with her big doe eyes and compact figure. It was not hard to imagine what she must have looked like as a young girl and to think of her lying in a rumpled bed after sex, stretching sinuously like a cat. Or maybe she was still a virgin after all these years, never having known a man in the biblical sense, shrivelling up as she grew older like an over-ripe fruit left untouched. Or maybe she had suffered a bad experience and turned to God as an alternative. A person's desire for religion, Fyfe could almost understand. But the parallel need for celibacy was totally beyond him.

The lift stopped with a soft bump. The doors pinged open and Miss Lyle led him out into a corridor lined with pictures of churches. Their footsteps made no sound on the thick carpet. A door at the end of the corridor stood open. She moved to one side and waved him on, taking his coat and draping it over her arm. He winked as he passed and she smiled. No virgin her, Fyfe decided. There was a lot of knowledge behind that smile, a lot of understanding. Some priest somewhere would have heard the details of her confession and dictated what penance she should do. No one else would ever know.

The room Fyfe went into was large with an old-fashioned marble fireplace straight ahead and windows on two sides making it almost uncomfortably bright. A tray with coffee and biscuits was on a low table circled by four chairs. The edge of the tray lay on a thin grey folder. Archbishop Delaney came out from behind his desk, holding out a hand in greeting. He was wearing a black suit and dog collar and there was a fresh scar on his chin where he had cut himself shaving that morning. Fyfe, already prejudiced after seeing his photograph downstairs, saw no reason to change his mind.

'Chief Inspector Fyfe. Glad you could come.'

'I just hope I can help.'

'So do I. So do I. You'll take some coffee? Or perhaps you would prefer tea? I tend to like very strong coffee.'

The offer was made in the spirit of a wine waiter who has opened the bottle and does not expect rejection. 'Coffee is fine,' Fyfe said, disappointed that he did not have the guts to be contrary.

'This is Mr Fleming, our accountant.'

A small, thin man was standing between the windows. Fyfe hadn't noticed him before. He was elderly and hunchbacked so that his head was permanently tilted to one side and one arm hung down towards the floor. He had huge ears and a flat nose. When God was handing out good looks, he had been trampled in the rush. When he shook hands his grip was limp and deferential. His doleful expression emphasised the gravity of the situation he had been responsible for uncovering. He took a cup of coffee and sat down in a chair at a slight remove from Fyfe and Delaney.

The Archbishop talked about the weather, inevitably, and then about his friend Sir Duncan, a charming bloke, and the lot of policemen generally, not a happy one. The conversation moved on seamlessly to moral standards, declining, and the prevalence of criminal behaviour, growing. He helped himself to a chocolate biscuit and decried the blatant materialistic tendencies of modern society.

'I held a Mass yesterday,' he said, staring blankly into the middle distance. 'It was in a church in a terribly poor part of the city. The people were poor. They have no money but they have rich souls. They may be at the bottom of the heap but they matter. Oh, how they matter.'

Fyfe sipped the bitter coffee and waited for the Archbishop to come out of his reverie, thinking that the Catholic Church was the biggest, most efficient money-making machine on earth and if it wasn't for the poor people it wouldn't be half so successful.

Don't be ungracious, he told himself. Would you condemn yourself to a lifetime of celibacy for a guaranteed supply of communion wine and chocolate biscuits? Certainly not. Fyfe cringed at the thought and felt his face colour when he began to wonder spontaneously if the Archbishop had ever slept with a woman. Delaney's head turned slowly towards him, eyes suddenly coming into focus.

'All right?' he inquired.

'What?'

'The coffee?'

'Fine. Just fine,' Fyfe assured him, taking another sip to demonstrate its acceptability.

Delaney laid down his own cup and saucer. He was coming to the point. The sermon was over and the moral message was next. Fleming rose to put his cup and saucer back on the tray. They rattled noisily.

'Sir Duncan has briefed you on our problem?' Delaney said.

'He has.'

The Archbishop nodded and his eyes took on a faraway look again. 'It is a terrible thing when the Church cannot trust its own people. The Church's money is God's money and a crime against the Church is a crime against God. A terrible thing.'

'Quite. Do you have any idea how much might be missing?'

'Several hundred thousand pounds, I am told, Chief Inspector. Something of that order. The exact figures and an explanation of the circumstances are in that folder there on the table.'

Fleming nodded in confirmation. Fyfe pretended not to be surprised at the amount of money involved. At the same time Delaney was shaking his head, making his jowls flop from side to side. 'It is, of course, as Sir Duncan will have told you, not the amount that matters — much of it is in tangible assets and can probably be recovered eventually. It is the breach of trust. You can imagine what a terrible discovery it was to make. I was physically sick when I realised what must have been happening.'

'I think I can imagine,' Fyfe said sympathetically. 'And you know the name of the bad apple in your barrel?'

Delaney's eyes snapped back into focus. 'Oh yes. Mr Fleming has singled out the culprit. There can be no doubt of his guilt although he continues to deny it. The evidence is set down in black and white. We have him bang to rights, as might be said in the vernacular.'

Fleming nodded again. His cloudy eyes threatened to rain tears.

'One of your priests, is he?' Fyfe said.

'I'm afraid so, Chief Inspector,' Delaney replied. 'Our Diocesan Chancellor, Father Richard Quinn.'

'What does Diocesan Chancellor mean?'

'He basically controls all the money that comes into the diocese. He pays the bills and underwrites charitable activities. He is, in effect, our banker. Every diocese has one.'

'Is he a trained accountant?'

'No. He just happens to be good with money. It would be ironic to call it a gift from God, but generally that is how our system works. Father Quinn is a man in his late fifties with a previously unblemished career. It grieves me terribly to find such self-seeking wickedness among men who are supposed to have pledged their life to God. It strikes at the very root of my faith in human nature.'

'It would do, wouldn't it? You are sure Quinn is guilty?'

'Totally convinced.'

'As guilty as sin, is he?' Fyfe could not resist saying.

'We're all sinners, Chief Inspector,' the Archbishop said, taking another chocolate biscuit. 'It is but a matter of degree. I retain a profound sense of compassion for a man who has succumbed to temptation in this way. Satan gloats over those who fall to temptation.'

'I take it you have confronted him with your version of events?'

'I have. It was a most unsettling experience.' Delaney wiped some crumbs from the corner of his mouth with his little finger.

'And his response?'

'He is unbalanced. He tried to blame it on the assistant priest in his parish, Father Donald Byrne. A most unsavoury attempt. The young priest was reduced to tears. It was he who came to me with the original suspicions that led to a closer examination of the figures. I have cross-examined him intensely and believe him to be innocent.'

'You remain convinced of Quinn's guilt?'

'I do and I have not arrived at that conclusion willingly. I am afraid it is inescapable. Mr Fleming is a parishioner of mine. He has confirmed it. I am no psychiatrist but I believe the extent of his guilt is of such enormity that he does not want to, cannot, face the truth.'

'There is the possibility that he may be innocent, of course. Perhaps this Father Byrne was involved.'

The Archbishop shook his head. 'The evidence in this case is overwhelming, as you will see, and there is none against Father Byrne. I have prayed that I should be wrong about Quinn but I do not think so. However, I realise that all human judgements are fallible.'

Except one, Fyfe thought disrespectfully. Maybe we should invite the Pope to give his infallible opinion. There was also the pertinent point that if Quinn was the wrong man the real embezzler was still at large.

'Father Quinn has lately been affected by a series of personal problems,' the Archbishop said. 'He has been seriously ill. I am sorry to say he started drinking heavily. If I sound harsh in my condemnation of him it is because I am disappointed his faith was not strong enough to support him.'

A whisky priest, Fyfe thought, trying to salt away some money for the long dark lonely days of his old age. Poor bastard would be too ashamed of what he had done to admit it.

'Of course,' he replied. 'I understand.'

'Anyway,' Delaney said, standing up, 'I discussed it with Duncan, Sir Duncan, and we agreed that the intervention of the police may extract the true story from him. The shock of an outside agency, someone not of the faith, may be enough to wring a confession from this man's tortured soul.'

'You mean do a deal with him?'

'The loss of his vocation will be punishment enough. The Church will be satisfied if we can get our money back. It may be recoverable, of course, through the science of accountancy because most of it apparently has been invested in stocks and shares and used to buy property. But if Father Quinn was to co-operate it would be recovered all the more speedily. I would hope to secure a withdrawal of his accusations against Father Byrne also.'

'This troublesome priest is causing you a lot of anguish.'

'He claims to be innocent of criminality. He says he will fight to clear his name but then contradicts himself by saying he only took the money to build an orphanage of all things in Eastern Europe.' Delaney exhaled like a man blowing up a balloon. 'I ask you. If this becomes public the shame could kill him. The embarrassment to the Church will be secondary.'

'Perhaps you need a psychiatrist rather than a policeman.'

'Perhaps. That will be our next step if you fail, Chief Inspector.'

Fyfe was not confident of success. If the perpetrator was not going to confess to a bloody Archbishop he was unlikely to be impressed by an agnostic detective.

'When can I see him?' he said. 'Where are you keeping him?'

Delaney clasped his hands behind his back where he stood beside the mantelpiece. 'He has agreed to stay at a retreat on Tayside run by one of our monastic orders. The rooms there are known as cells. An apt description. He will not be going anywhere until this matter is settled. I have taken possession of his passport. You can see him this afternoon.'

Fyfe acknowledged a grudging flicker of respect for Delaney's pragmatic attitude. Muscular Christianity it might be called. Delaney kept repeating that he was more worried about the man than the money but that was purely for form's sake. Quinn had been caught and was not going to be allowed to get away.

'I went to my friend Sir Duncan for advice and he recommended you, Chief Inspector. We hope you can have some effect on this poor unfortunate, that you can somehow draw the poison from his soul. Of course, you will appreciate the delicacy of the situation. Only I and Mr Fleming and the assistant priest Byrne so far know what has transpired and that is the way it should remain. Let us keep this private.'

'Just between us,' Fyfe said, remembering Miss Lyle who had buried four Archbishops.

'Free will is a cross humans have to bear. We must be responsible for our actions and pay the price of repentance.'

Fyfe sensed the interview was coming to a close and stood up. 'Obviously, I cannot guarantee that there will be no proceedings in this case. If a crime has been committed, the law may have to take its course.'

'Chief Inspector Fyfe, I understand perfectly. The Church, too, has its laws. They must not be ignored and they must be interpreted correctly or all is chaos.'

They shook hands, Delaney maintaining his grip for longer than was necessary. Fleming also offered his hand and a business card.

'I do not have to tell you that the fewer people who know about this the better,' Delaney said. 'For the time being at least. Call me and keep me appraised of any progress.'

'You can trust me, Archbishop.'

'Let us hope we can restore a little justice to our hugely imperfect world. Miss Lyle will show you out. She has the address of the retreat for you. It is less than two hours' drive, somewhere north of Dundee.'

Miss Lyle appeared at the door on cue, holding his coat. Fyfe had not noticed Delaney do anything that might have summoned her. He repeated his goodbyes and took the folder, rolling it into a tube to carry it in one hand. Miss Lyle led him to the lift in silence. Inside she handed him a single sheet of paper with an address and phone number on it.

'It's a Cistercian order,' she said. 'Not a very talkative lot.'

Fyfe grinned and saw his twin reflections smile back from the convex lenses of her glasses. At ground level the doors pinged open and he stepped out past Miss Lyle. She reached out and touched his sleeve.

'Go get him, boy,' she said. 'May Our Lady watch over you.'

14

Billy Jones drummed his fingers impatiently on the steering wheel of the van and stared at the pub entrance. He chewed the last of a takeaway bacon roll and dropped its wrapping on the floor beside the polystyrene cups and other debris. His brother Sandy sat beside him, reading a copy of the *Daily Record* and mindlessly humming the latest chart-climbing pop tune.

'Shut up, will you?' Billy shouted, chopping down through the newspaper with the side of his hand.

'Fuck's sake, Billy. There's no need for that,' he said, trying to reassemble the torn paper. 'There's only one way in and out. We'll get the bastard soon enough. Loosen up.'

Sandy shook his head and pulled nervously at his earring. 'It's been too long. What do you think they're doing in there?'

'What people usually do in pubs. Picking their noses.'

'I don't like it when priests get involved in our business.'

'He's not involved. We wait until he moves out of the picture and then lift Adamson. He won't be involved.'

'Supposing they seek sanctuary in a church?'

Sandy giggled. He smoothed out the sports pages of the newspaper and began reading again.

'What happens if the priest doesn't leave him? Supposing they stay together all night? What do we do then?'

'We'll just have to lift both of them,' Sandy said without looking up.

'Oh no. Oh no. I'm not topping any priest. I'm not having anything to do with that.'

'You going to tell the boss of your sudden attack of conscience?'

Billy leaned forward and bumped his forehead off the windscreen three times. He snatched the newspaper from Sandy, shredded it and tossed it over his shoulder into the back of the van. Then he slapped his brother on the back of the head. Sandy slapped him back. Billy pressed the palm of his hand against Sandy's nose. Sandy twisted his head away and tried to grab Billy's wrist.

'I don't like it,' Billy said, backing off.

'I don't like the fucking weather but there's bugger all I can do about it,' Sandy replied. 'We need Adamson. If the priest gets in the way we can nudge him gently to the side. We don't have to hurt him.'

'We could hurt him just a little bit.'

'Whatever's necessary. Let's wait and see.'

Sandy rescued a page of the newspaper and began reading again. Billy leaned over the wheel and rested his forehead on the windscreen. He stiffened when he saw Adamson emerge from the pub. Byrne was right behind him, putting on his dog collar.

'Waiting's over,' Billy said.

15

Fyfe went to the local police station in Leith after his meeting with Archbishop Delaney. It was a converted town hall full of dark wood panelling and high ceilings. From there he phoned the retreat on the Tayside coast. Brother Patrick answered and confirmed he was expected. Complicated directions to get there by road were repeated twice.

'Out here in the back of beyond we are very hard to find,' Brother Patrick said. 'Isn't it marvellous?'

Fyfe agreed. He wrote down the information and checked the route on a road map that gave no indication of the existence of the place. Then he read over the report prepared by the taciturn accountant Fleming. It was pretty damning. The main scam was to have a legitimate Church drug rehabilitation project pay cash into a bank account as rent for accommodation which already belonged to the Church and wages for employees who did not exist. Cheques drawn on the account had bought jewellery, membership of a book club and numerous cases of expensive claret among other assorted items, the most exotic of which was a silver-plated chess set with pieces representing Satanic and Heavenly forces. A full-page advertisement for the set torn from a glossy magazine was included in the file. Nice touch, Fyfe thought, warming to the deviant sense of humour that could do such perversely flippant things.

The cheques and credit card slips were signed with Richard Quinn's name, less his holy designation. Quinn, naturally, was the leader of the rehabilitation project. Comparative handwriting samples left little doubt who had written the signatures, apart from some that were illegible scrawls. Amounts of two hundred and fifty pounds had also been withdrawn in cash at regular, almost daily, intervals on a cash card dedicated to Quinn. Only eighteen thousand out of the hundreds of thousands of pounds was unaccounted for. Fleming had nailed the swindler good and proper.

'Not much imagination, Father Quinn, apart from the chess set,' Fyfe said. 'Looks like an open and shut case. I wonder what you've got to say for yourself.'

Jewellery. The idea of a priest buying women's jewellery intrigued him. Did that mean Quinn was helping himself to some of the pleasures of the flesh at the same time he was ripping off his Church? What a hypocrite, but as well to be hung for a sheep as a lamb. Fyfe shook his head and grinned, conjuring up a mental picture of a naked priest wearing nothing but a dog collar separated from a naked woman wearing nothing but a crucifix by a table supporting the silver chess set. The priest fingered his Satanic king considering his next move while the woman anxiously surveyed her flights of defending angels. 'Checkmate,' the priest would whisper when he finally made his move.

Fyfe decided he would drop in by the priest's house to see if Quinn's assistant was around. It was on his way out of the city and if there was no one there he would try again the next day. It might be useful to get a perspective on the man and what might be expected. It would be interesting to see what a close colleague's view of his outrageous behaviour would be. All forgiveness and understanding probably, unlike the Archbishop.

Fyfe shared some gossip with the duty inspector. Another two murders reported that morning, both garrotted like the dead man on Portobello beach. Cheese wire slicing through skin and blood and bone, a drug war trademark. It looked like a particularly nasty falling out among criminals. Fyfe felt a brief twinge of envy for whoever would be in charge of the case but didn't let it show. Real crime, a real touch of malice. Juicy stuff. The media were howling for action. There was a rumour that everyone was going to be told to drop everything and work on the case. Fyfe checked the pager on his belt. They knew how to get him when they needed him.

He drove to the church. It was on the border between an exclusive leafy area of big trees, big houses, and big gardens, and a sprawling council-built estate where the satellite dishes sprouted like mushrooms from the rows of window-dotted walls. The building was a relatively recent concrete monstrosity, all clashing curves and soaring verticals and rain-stained concrete panels. Scaffolding covered one wall with a huge banner advertising the building firm, Windfall Construction, tied to it.

The priest's house was tacked on at the rear, a bit like a lean-to shed. Fyfe knocked and waited. An elderly woman opened the door, wiping her hands on an apron and peering suspiciously at him. There was a wedding ring that was too big for a bony finger. No other jewellery except gold ear studs. Little make-up. The only real concession to vanity was a permed hair-style so perfect it might have been a wig. It wasn't though. The blue-tinged roots came from the scalp. Definitely a widow, this one, Fyfe thought. The faith had need of an endless supply. Where did they find them all?

'Can I help you?' she asked.

'I was hoping for a word with Father...' The name escaped him for a few seconds and he felt stupid, annoyed at his amateurism. 'Father Byrne. Is he here at the moment?'

'I'm afraid not.'

'Pity. I'm Chief Inspector Fyfe. I need to talk to him.'

'Oh.' The housekeeper seemed to grow taller, squaring up as if ready to fight. Her mouth grew smaller, her chest bigger. 'The police.'

'Yes. I have a few questions to ask.'

'I suppose you do,' she agreed, relaxing and shrinking. 'Well, the Father will be back at any moment. I thought it was him at the door when you knocked. Would you like to wait?'

'No. I'll come back tomorrow.'

'I'm sure he won't be long.'

He looked past her along the corridor and saw into a study crammed with books on sagging shelves and an ancient mahogany breakfront bookcase with leaded glass doors that was out of all proportion to the size of the room. Cardboard boxes full of papers were stacked up against the walls. A window looked out on a lawn. The grass needed cutting.

'Will you tell him I'd like a word, Mrs...?'

'Of course. The name is Mrs McMorrow.'

'Mrs McMorrow. He'll probably know what it's about.'

'I'm sure he will. It's about Father Quinn, isn't it?'

'That's right. I suppose you were Father Quinn's housekeeper too?'

'Oh yes. I was with him in his last parish. This church is only a few years old. The last one burned down. You can see that they're still building it. It was meant to be finished two years ago.'

'You know him well, then?'

She nodded thoughtfully and lifted her head to stare at Fyfe. 'I know him well,' she said defiantly.

'It would come as a great surprise, then. This trouble over this money.'

'A surprise? Yes. I'm surprised that people who should know better think the worst of Father Quinn.'

Fyfe hesitated, wondering how much fact and rumour were intertwined in her understanding of the affair, how much loyalty blinded her to the reality. Fyfe pulled his coat tighter around him and tried to think of a polite excuse to end the conversation and get away.

'I know it's no business of mine,' said Mrs McMorrow in a tone that implied it should be. 'But I think it is disgraceful the way Father Quinn is being treated. A man is innocent until he is proved guilty, isn't he? Isn't that the way it works?'

'Definitely,' Fyfe agreed. 'That's the way it works.'

'Then why have they locked him away?'

'He's at a retreat. No one forced him to go.'

Mrs McMorrow looked at him and the corner of her top lip twitched as though she was going to growl like a dog. Fyfe felt a mild blush spread over his face. When she shook her head almost imperceptibly in sad recognition of his naïvety he blushed even more. Her head was suddenly shaking violently, her eyes blinking. It continued to shake for several seconds, slowing down like a clockwork toy. She looked as if she was about to burst into tears. The poor woman must have had the last of her illusions shattered when Quinn was found out. The person she had chosen to invest her emotions in, whom she had looked after, respected and trusted for so many years, had turned out to be a crook. The man who must have been a combination of father, son, husband and brother to her had lied repeatedly, abused her trust and betrayed her loyalty. No wonder she refused to believe it.

'Well, I must be going,' Fyfe said. 'Please tell Father Byrne I'll be back tomorrow.'

'Tell him yourself,' Mrs McMorrow replied. 'Here he is now.'

Fyfe turned and saw an athletic man get out of an old car with rust streaks along the wing. His hair was slightly dishevelled, eyes staring slightly, like a villainous character from a Victorian melodrama if it wasn't for the dog collar. He didn't try to hide his irritation until Fyfe introduced himself. Then an artificial smile flickered momentarily and changed into a grave expression more suiting to the occasion. This guy's a gold-plated hypocrite, Fyfe thought. I wouldn't trust him with the collection money.

'Chief Inspector, I'm afraid this is a bad time. Bit of an emergency on at the moment. Can't stop. Got a problem in the car that won't wait. Sorry about this. I don't mean to be rude.'

Byrne brushed past Fyfe and Mrs McMorrow and disappeared into the study. He searched in the drawers of the bookcase. Mrs McMorrow's face was completely blank. Fyfe looked back at the car to see who was the origin of the priestly emergency. There was somebody in the passenger seat, keeping his head down, one hand covering his eyes.

Byrne came rushing out, stuffing something into his pocket. 'It is important that we talk fully on this matter,' he said. 'But I don't have time just now. There are souls to save out there, you know.'

'I know. I know.'

'Tomorrow?'

'Fine. I'll come back.'

Byrne hurried on to join the sinner in his car. Fyfe instantly decided that he did not like this priest, sensing a zealot who enjoyed seeing the downfall of others because it confirmed his own cleverness in avoiding such a fate in the material world. By comparison, Father Quinn's feet of clay were a much more attractive prospect. Let him who is without sin cast the first stone and all that kind of stuff.

The sinner kept his head bowed, rubbing the bridge of his nose so that his face was obscured. An adulterer, Fyfe speculated? Or an abortionist? Or just somebody who hadn't been to church for a while? A breaker of the religious rules anyway. A soul to be saved.

The car drove off, spewing oil-blackened smoke from its exhaust.

'Busy man, your Father Byrne,' Fyfe said to Mrs McMorrow who was still standing in the doorway. 'I'll catch him later.'

'Yes. That will be best.'

'I'm going to see Father Quinn now. Any messages for him?'

'Tell him I still believe in him if nobody else does,' she said.

'You believe he is innocent, don't you?'

'I know who is responsible for all these goings on.'

'You do? Tell me then.'

She looked away from him towards a patch of grass dividing the church grounds from the main road where wind-blown litter gathered itself into a tidy pile against a fence. Three metal tree guards stood in a line on the grass. None of them contained a tree.

'Don't you understand?' she asked, genuinely puzzled. 'Isn't it obvious? Can't you see?'

'Who?'

'The Devil, that's who. It is all the Devil's work.'

16

'Who the fuck was that?' Adamson demanded, looking back unnecessarily once the car was round a corner. 'I know him. He's a policeman, isn't he?'

Byrne worked hard at remaining calm, forcing his expression into a fixed smile. He had been expecting the police for a while now. He had discussed it with the Archbishop and prepared his reaction carefully. It was unfortunate they should decide to show up at this particular moment, just when he was about to collect the main prize. It was unfortunate that he had gone back to get the spending money he had promised Adamson, having forgotten it that morning. Adamson had been resigned and compliant before but now he had suddenly become agitated and upset.

'He's a fucking policeman. I recognise him. He was one of the ones that arrested me. He kept chucking questions at me in the nick. What's his name?'

'Detective Chief Inspector Fyfe, I believe.'

'That's him. Fyfe. A real smart bastard. He had this trick of massaging your shoulders, real friendly like, then he dug in his thumbs.'

'You remember him after nine years?'

'I remember everything about that day. I carry it around with me like a bloody photograph album. I remember Fyfe all right. What's he doing here?'

'It's unrelated. A totally different matter. Pure coincidence.'

The church was out of sight. Adamson turned round, shaking his head. His hair touched the roof and stuck there, held by static electricity.

'It's too much of a coincidence. They must be watching me. They have been waiting till I get out in the hope that I'll lead them straight to the cash. They must have followed me.'

'No,' Byrne insisted, worried by the simplicity of the interconnecting logic. 'It is nothing to do with you. It is something totally different, I assure you.'

Byrne saw Adamson's eyes narrow, his forehead wrinkle, his expression darken. He was assessing the options, trying to think it through. Maybe he was right, Byrne thought nervously. Was it too much of a coincidence?

'Why would Fyfe make himself obvious like that?' Byrne asked, trying to convince himself. 'If he was following you he would surely have waited until you had your hands on the cash before making his move. Why would he show his hand just now?'

'Exactly. Why would he?'

'Because it has nothing to do with you. He came to see me on an unrelated matter. It is a coincidence. It is.'

'What was it?'

'Somebody I know who got into trouble over money. Different money.'

'What about the sanctity of the confessional?'

'It wasn't a parishioner. It was a colleague.'

'A colleague? You mean a priest?'

'Yes. A fellow priest.'

Byrne almost choked on the words as he said them. His confidence in the efficacy of his plan waned suddenly and dramatically. He had wanted to reassure Adamson that Fyfe wasn't a danger but hadn't meant to tell him so much. Too late now, he realised. His hold over Adamson was slipping. His controlling influence was being swamped by the rush of warm blood that made his face glow red.

'Jesus Christ,' Adamson said slowly. 'Another fucking crooked priest. Is nothing sacred any more? What has happened to the world since I left it?'

Byrne didn't say anything. The skin crawled unpleasantly on the back of his neck and his intestines coiled into an uncomfortably tight knot. The altered tone of Adamson's voice was like a razor blade slicing across the surface of his brain. Their relationship had changed totally in the space of a few minutes. Superior and subordinate had switched places. He no longer dictated what was to happen but instead had become a martyr to the circumstances he had created. It must be God's will, he thought objectively, and a partially stifled upswelling of laughter made his body shudder.

'Stop the car,' Adamson said.

Byrne obeyed without protest. He felt hollow, his skin so fragile that a finger poked against it would go right through. When Adamson patted him gently on the arm the slight pressure was like a blow with a heavy hammer.

He winced involuntarily. Adamson took the envelope and removed four five-pound notes from it.

'I've got to think,' Adamson said, getting out of the car.

65

'But what about our arrangement?' Byrne pleaded.

'I'll see you later tonight. At the flat. I've got to have time to think.'

17

Billy Jones stopped the van the length of the street behind Byrne's car and shook his brother Sandy awake.

'He's getting out,' Billy shouted. 'Get after him.'

Sandy was slow to grasp what was happening when he woke up. His neck was stiff and there was no feeling in the arm he had squashed beneath him in the passenger seat. 'What's going on?' he asked stupidly.

Billy leaned across and opened the van door. 'Adamson is doing a runner. Get on his tail.'

Sandy looked ahead and summed up the situation. He saw Adamson beginning to move away from the car and a belch of black smoke from its exhaust as it pulled back into the traffic. He sighed.

'It's fucking cold out there.'

'You stick with Adamson. One of us needs to be on foot. I'll stay with the van.'

'But it's cold.'

'Get out, you useless jessie. We'll snatch him at the first opportunity but remember, we don't want any witnesses.'

Sandy slid reluctantly out of his seat and on to the road. He cowered by the door for a few seconds and zipped the leather jacket all the way up to his neck. The rain licked at his face.

'Don't do anything without my say-so,' Billy said. 'Just don't lose him. Phone me on the mobile when we can take him.'

Sandy plunged his hands deep into his pockets and hunched his shoulders. 'All right for you, you bastard,' he muttered. 'How come you get to stay nice and warm? Thanks for the chance to freeze my balls off.'

'That's what brothers are for.'

Sandy walked round to the pavement. In the distance Adamson was turning a corner. Sandy stopped grumbling and broke into a shambling trot to catch up.

18

Fyfe drove north from Edinburgh. The city was shrouded in a grey afternoon fog. Buildings bobbed about in it like flotsam drifting in the sea. A cold sun shone above it like an under-powered light bulb in a smoke-filled room. A drizzle of rain fell steadily. He paid the toll at the barrier of the Forth Bridge and quickly wound up the window to keep out the slimy wet air. He passed under the giant suspension towers that disappeared into the amorphous greyness above. Over the bridge and on to the Perth motorway and the susurrus of overtaking cars became a hypnotic sound.

He had to drive slowly. The car, like his thoughts, was cocooned in a little bubble of clarity surrounded by the fog. The dampness of the air translated itself into individual droplets that trembled on the bonnet and queued up at the edge of the windscreen like beads on an abacus. He ran the heating at full blast. The radio played loud music.

He thought about corrupt priests in long robes and Sylvia, the avaricious advocate, parading before him shamelessly in nothing but her wig and gown. He thought of how Lord Greenmantle's scrawny neck rubbed against his stiff collar and how he had once held Fyfe back in the witness box after cross-examination in a trial.

'You are absolutely sure, are you, Sergeant Fyfe?' he had asked, writing furiously.

'Yes, my Lord.'

'Absolutely sure?'

The repetition of the question implied doubt. Fyfe's hesitation enhanced the implication. Everyone in the courtroom was looking at him. None of them had pity in their eyes.

'Absolutely sure, my Lord,' he said louder than necessary.

He could remember only the exchange with Greenmantle, not the details of the trial or even what it was he had been so absolutely sure about. It was a small incident contained inside its own little bubble of clarity and it had prejudiced him against Greenmantle for ever. His engagement to Sylvia prejudiced him even more.

'Absolutely sure, my Lord,' he said, grinning foolishly at the reflection of his eyes in the rear-view mirror. 'Absolutely sure that I have slept with your future wife. No question. Absolutely sure.'

He thought about Mrs McMorrow's simple view of life which avoided all personal responsibility, and he imagined the three near-decapitated bodies now lying on mortuary slabs in the city behind him. Whose fault was that? The Devil did indeed work in mysterious ways.

The car suddenly popped like a cork from the fog into bright sunshine. Fyfe shaded his eyes, lowered the sun visor and pressed the accelerator pedal to the floor.

19

Adamson walked erect, ignoring the rain. The high buildings on either side seemed to lean inwards threateningly towards him but he refused to be intimidated. He passed the roller shutters of the tattoo shop, and the Barnardo's, and the 99p Wonderland, and the kebab takeaway, and the patterned wrought-iron work on the head-high windows of the Ranch Bar. Every second shop was boarded up and plastered with torn and fading posters. A new poster outside a newsagent's announced a Double Murder Riddle.

It was all so familiar, barely changed at all. Even the litter in the gutters, trapped around the wheels of the unbroken line of cars, looked the same as it had nine years before when he and Mike came charging along after being spotted. The sirens had been squealing after them as they knocked pedestrians out of the way in what he had assumed was to be their last desperate attempt to escape capture. They were running into a hopeless dead end. He had not known then just how desperate Mike was. Mike had decided to escape whatever happened. He had his own personal escape route.

The first-floor flat had belonged to a friend. There was nowhere else to go. Luckily for the friend he wasn't there. They had battered the door in and then barricaded it and Mike had started blasting out the window. Five hours it lasted. They had seen themselves on the television. Then it was all over. Mike used the last cartridge on himself. His blood was everywhere. So were the police.

The flat was above the same fruit and vegetable shop. There was a light on in the room behind closed curtains. A Chicago Bears American football sticker was on one corner of the window. Adamson stood staring up at it, feeling warm air blow in his face from the pub vents, hearing the hum of voices from the interior. He stood there for five minutes, feeling a satisfying sense of achievement. Nine years, he told himself, and the bastards still can't be sure what happened to the money. The secret is mine, all mine, and no one else is going to get their hands on it.

It had been with a sense of relief that Adamson had seen the detective David Fyfe at the church house when Father Byrne had gone back to get him some spending money. It had given him an excuse to call off the supposed recovery of the cash. He had been stringing Byrne along without a clear idea of what he was going to do when it came to the crunch. He would look such a fool if he produced nothing to hand over. Byrne would laugh at him. Adamson couldn't permit that. He wouldn't let himself be made out to be a fool.

Fyfe had acted the good guy policeman for a while after his arrest, guiding him into the back seat of the patrol car with a blanket over his head, checking that the handcuffs were not too tight, supplying tea and cigarettes and sympathy. But he quickly lost patience with the softly-softly approach and started his painful thumb-gouging trick. Then he seemed to lose the place altogether and kicked the legs from under the chair so that Adamson banged the back of his head on the floor when he fell.

That shut his mouth tight. If he had been left another five minutes he might have told the whole story, given it all away. He had been close to breaking point but Fyfe had spoiled it.

Nine years ago, that had been. He had got back into the chair and looked over at Fyfe and could see that he appreciated exactly what had happened. Funny how Fyfe should appear now, allowing him to get away from the clutches of Father Byrne, at least temporarily while he sorted himself out. A coincidence, Byrne had said. A happy coincidence. Even if Fyfe was looking for him to check up on the money, it would do him no good. But it was nice to feel wanted.

Adamson abruptly turned away from his position in the street below the window of the flat. He didn't want to draw attention to himself by loitering too obviously. He began retracing his steps, visualising himself and Mike Barrie running wildly. He reached the corner and looked along the next street where most of the tenements had been pulled down and replaced by more modern, terraced and detached housing. They had run along here too. Then it had been a construction site for most of its length, dotted with heaps of sand and piles of bricks and an estate of half-built houses. There had been a chain link fence and notices warning of guard dogs. And it had been a Sunday and no one was working. They had counted the money inside a house with plastic sheeting for windows and sawdust all over the bare floorboards.

Adamson walked slowly, looking at the houses with their orange roof tiles and plumes of pampas grass on tiny patches of front garden. He superimposed his memory of the building site on the actuality in front of him and the two images merged. But he could not decide where the house had been. Presumably it had been rebuilt after the fire, the ashes swept away and the gap filled. He had tried but he could not remember exactly.

He stopped. This was where it had all gone wrong. It was here they had been seen by a policeman on the beat, standing in the street talking like two long-lost friends. Stupid with hindsight for them both to have gone to collect the car. Stupid to hang around trying to look casual. But then it had been stupid for Adamson to go along with Mike's plan to booby trap the money, to stack it so carefully and place the candle in its dish of petrol. 'No bastard but us is sharing this,' he had said. 'If we can't have it, no one else is.' And Adamson didn't have the guts to argue. Stupid. So stupid.

The policeman had shouted. They had run. Mike had died. He had survived. The booby trap had been sprung. Nine years later he had returned, having kept the faith. A long time. A very long time.

Adamson started walking again. He didn't look back. He would find a pub. Drink a couple of pints. Give himself time to think. But he had already made up his mind what he had to do. He wasn't going to act stupid this time. No one was going to make a fool of him.

20

Fyfe slowed his car and drew to a halt in a passing place. He got out to look, shading his eyes against the glare of the cold, rain-shot sunlight. Fields and bare moorland and stunted forests dipped and curved all around him in a vast bowl of undulating land. A thin V-shaped wedge had been broken off one side of the bowl and was filled by the sea. He had asked for directions in the village several miles back and been sent on to the narrow road with crumbling edges that took him, all of a sudden, into a desolate environment he could hardly have guessed was within a few minutes' drive of ordinary civilisation. He had listened to an excitable radio reporter rant on about drug wars in Edinburgh with three murders in one night. A climate of terror had gripped the city, she said breathlessly. Fyfe's pager remained silent.

The road ran away from where he stood, unexpectedly straight, like a crack across the surface of brown heather and green grass, between the shining flecks of exposed rock. Sheep were sparsely irregular white specks on the hillsides. Herds of deer were up there too probably, camouflaged and invisible to his city-trained eye, but he knew they were there because he had seen them. The approach of his car had disturbed them as they foraged near the roadside and they had turned and galloped off, merging completely with the landscape within a few hundred yards.

The directions were quite specific. Drive five miles up the single track that branches off the metalled road and find a rough track on the left just beyond the second cattle grid. Drive slowly over it or it will rip off your exhaust, and you will find the monks' retreat on the coast about a mile further on. Don't worry if you can't see the building and think you are heading into the middle of nowhere. It is only visible for the last few hundred yards. Have faith and you will find us, the jovial Brother Patrick had assured him. We don't get many visitors.

Looking down, Fyfe could see where tyre tracks had flattened the verge and led on to a track that was barely distinguishable from the general spread of grass and scattered boulders. The faint impression of the track pointed towards the sea, indicating the correct direction. It had to be the right place. Have faith, Fyfe thought. Rely on your Boy Scout training.

He sucked in a long breath of fresh air and enjoyed the stimulating coldness of it inflating his lungs. Then he got back into his car. It bumped off the smooth road on to the rock-strewn track. Soon it became obvious that he would not be able to change out of second gear or build up any speed. The car lurched and dropped as if it was a ship negotiating the peaks and troughs of a slow motion stormy sea. Fyfe had to use all his concentration to avoid the worst of the obstacles, terrified that he would scrape the sump and be left stranded with nothing but wilderness and peat bog surrounding him. It would be a very long hike back.

It took him thirty minutes to cover two miles and there was still nothing to be seen. He began to curse savagely out loud, convinced he had taken the wrong route, trying to work out how he could turn round, when he topped a crest and saw the retreat directly ahead of him. It was a large, many-windowed house with a pepper-pot turret on one corner of the steeply pitched roof and a square tower on the other, each sprouting unused flag-poles. Between them was a row of half a dozen gargoyles. A hooded monk was standing motionless on the steps beside the ten-foot-high front door that was flanked by a pair of recumbent stone lions. The monk wore a traditional off-white habit with a plaited cord tied round his waist. He held his hands crossed into opposite sleeves.

The scene was, at first glance, a disconcerting throwback to medieval times. Fyfe's initial impression was to imagine himself caught in a time warp. He must have passed through a portal, so beloved of science fiction writers, somewhere in the remote countryside and unknowingly travelled back to a different age. But as the novelty of the thought wiped the frown from his face and turned it into an amused smile, he was noticing give-away evidence of truly modern influences. There was glass in the windows, and an electric fence surrounding vegetable gardens that occupied a site about fifty yards to one side. Another monk in hood and habit was bent over the engine of a bright red miniature tractor. At its rear a shiny rotavator dripped black earth. Three black and white dairy cows, with heavy swollen udders, had yellow plastic tags in their ears. A tall aerial projected from the roof of the house, seeming to spring from the head of the most hideous gargoyle, rising like a jet of water and just starting to fall back on itself where it ended. The monk by the door stepped forward as Fyfe parked the car close to the steps. Ankle-high Reebok trainers appeared below the hem of the monk's robe.

'It's my corns, before you ask,' the monk said, pushing back the hood to reveal a round, almost bald head with grey eyes and the squashed features of a former boxer. He held out one leg in front of him like a dancer performing. 'These soft protective shoes are a luxury I regret and also covet. I am a poor Christian, a poorer monk. I am more concerned about the state of my temporal feet than the state of my immortal soul. How can I presume to be a proper example for mankind?'

'Brother Patrick?' Fyfe said.

'The same.'

They shook hands and the monk touched Fyfe's shoulders like a tailor finishing the fitting for a new suit.

'Nice place you have here,' Fyfe said.

'A folly, like all human life,' Brother Patrick explained with an all-encompassing wave of his arm. 'It was built more than a hundred years ago by an English factory owner who wanted to live in seclusion, ministered to by the comforts of his wealth rather than the company of his fellow man. When he died, alone and friendless, he bequeathed it to our order as a kind of atonement for his exploitation of people during his life. Probably believed it would buy him a place in heaven.'

'And did it?'

'If only it was as easy as that, Chief Inspector Fyfe. If only.'

Brother Patrick smiled sadly and turned to lead the way inside. He limped despite the Reeboks that padded silently over the bare wooden floorboards, and he talked like a tour guide on automatic pilot. They were a community of eight monks, providing retreats for those seeking spiritual guidance in their lives. They had an arrangement with the neighbouring estate owner to use his Range Rover to get people and supplies in and out. There was a phone to contact the outside world, a radio to keep up with the news, and a bedroom converted into a chapel for devotions. The rest, he said solemnly, is silence.

Fyfe looked out the window of the drawing-room. The house was constructed so that its walls rose directly from a sheer cliff face. Below was a small natural harbour and quayside, rusty iron rings still embedded in the rock above a fringe of clinging green seaweed. A path of irregular carved steps followed the contours upwards.

'On stormy days with an easterly wind the sea spray hammers against this window,' Brother Patrick said. 'Sometimes you expect the waves to come crashing right through. We were bequeathed the furniture as well.'

He flapped an arm at the antique sideboards and bookcases and the huge bow-legged table in the middle of the room. Gilt-framed portraits of anonymous people lined the walls. There was the impression of disuse and dust, cobwebs in dark corners, and a faintly unpleasant smell. Fyfe thought that if he listened hard enough he should be able to hear woodworm boring into the ancient wood.

'It is serviceable,' Brother Patrick said. 'At least the toilets are state of the art. The last thing we had repaired. Now, if you will wait here I will tell Father Quinn you have arrived.'

'Can you tell me anything about Father Quinn before I meet him?' Fyfe said hurriedly. 'Has he said anything to you?'

'No,' Brother Patrick said blankly.

'Oh, I'm sorry. I thought you must be aware of the circumstances.'

'All I know is that Father Quinn is considered a suicide risk. We watch him carefully.'

'Is he? I didn't realise.'

'Suicide is a mortal sin. We try to dissuade him. We try to remind him that God has purpose for every life.'

'Is suicide a worse sin than the one that brought him here?'

A sad smile twitched over Brother Patrick's face. 'I keep a small stone on my bedside table, Chief Inspector.'

'Do you?' said Fyfe, confused.

'I keep it there as a reminder.'

'A reminder of what?' Fyfe asked.

'That it should only be cast by those without sin.' He put his hands inside the opposite sleeves of his habit and limped off silently. 'I will get Father Quinn for you now.'

21

Father Donald Byrne was in an ugly mood when he barged straight into Lillian's flat without knocking. She was stretched out on the sofa in T-shirt and jeans watching the afternoon soaps. She pretended not to notice that he had arrived but her curiosity got the better of her when he grabbed the half-bottle of whisky she was using to treat a mild toothache and started knocking it back.

'Hard day at the office?' she said sarcastically.

'Shut up,' he snapped.

Lillian watched the television screen. He was a reflection on it, standing behind her. He was breathing heavily from the climb up the stairs and his dog collar was slightly askew like a hoop thrown over a target head at a fun-fair. He started to change into his track suit and jogging shoes. Lillian groaned inwardly, realising what that meant for her.

'Where's the pal you were bringing back to be my next-door neighbour?' she asked.

'He'll be here,' Byrne replied.

'When?'

'Soon.'

'That's all right then. Should I warm his slippers?'

'Shut up.'

Lillian did as she was told. Byrne could be a violent bastard. He had hit her before. The small piece of scar tissue above her left eye was his handiwork. She could sense that he was close to striking out now as a nervous response to whatever had angered him. She did not want to provoke him so she kept quiet, concentrating on following the story of the soap. Byrne crouched down behind the sofa. Only his head was visible, hooded now, a skull-like wraith on the screen. She felt his hand begin to stroke her hair gently. It moved on to her shoulder and down her arm. With the palm of his hand he began to caress a breast through the material of her T-shirt, gaining urgency with each circular motion. Shit, she thought. No rest for the wicked.

22

So this was the wicked Father Quinn. An old man with a pot-belly, rounded shoulders, slightly protruding eyes, and a deeply lined face that looked as if it had just been pressed hard up against the mesh of a wire grille. There were tufts of grey-brown hair on his scalp and in his nostrils and ears. His nose was squashed to one side and huge ear lobes hung like pieces of fleshy jewellery, engorged with bright pink blood. The edge of his mouth was slightly turned down on the left, suggesting a mild stroke, and the tip of his tongue continually poked in and out of it. He was wearing a plain grey jogging suit. His footwear was of a much cheaper variety than the Reeboks on Brother Patrick who stood in the doorway for a moment as Quinn entered and then disappeared.

Father Quinn walked across the creaking floorboards towards Fyfe, somehow managing to take a seat beside him at the table without once looking at him.

'I am Detective Chief Inspector David Fyfe, Father.'

Quinn sat with his arms folded, head to one side, staring out through the triptych of arched windows at the sea. The daylight was beginning to fail and the clean straight line of the horizon to fade. He made no attempt to introduce himself or say anything. Fyfe followed his gaze, trying to think of a good way of beginning the conversation. He had nothing prepared, no carefully thought out line of questioning. He was only there because the Chief Constable was a pal of the Archbishop. Did it really matter that Quinn had nicked the money? He wouldn't do it again, wouldn't get the chance. The Roman Catholic Church could afford it. A few thousand pounds out of a hole in its pocket wasn't going to bankrupt the Vatican. Why not let the poor old bastard be tortured by his conscience for the rest of his miserable life? Wouldn't a few hundred Hail Marys suffice? Was it really necessary to force an old man into a soul-destroying admission of iniquity?

'Okay, I give in. I can't take this silence any longer. I'll admit to anything.'

Fyfe was surprised by the outburst. He had been lulled into a near-hypnotic trance by watching the motion of the sea against the rocks outside. It hadn't been an intentional tactic to break the ice but it seemed to have worked. He turned to Quinn, who was sitting with his hands on his knees and his belly sagging low between them. He might have been smiling but it was hard to tell because of the lop-sided nature of his face. Every breath was a laboured wheeze. He had a deep voice that whistled on sibilant letters and created a row of tiny bubbles on his bottom lip. There were no nails on three of the fingers of his right hand.

'Did you steal the money?' Fyfe asked.

'No.'

'None at all?'

'I wanted a set of strips for the Sunday league football team I ran. I couldn't get official approval. They said it was too much of an extravagance. An extravagance, by God. For some of my boys it would have been the first new piece of clothing they had ever pulled over their head. Anyway, I decided to take an executive decision and allocated the money myself. Is that stealing?'

'Probably not.'

'Then there were a mountain of other things that needed buying so I bought them, some of them. All of a sudden a few thousand pounds had vanished from the accounts.'

'What did you buy?'

'Stuff for the boys. We hired a bus and went on a tour to Spain. Didn't cost them a penny and they loved it. I'm good with figures. I could have been an accountant. At the levels I stuck to, the Church never knew where the money went and the boys appreciated it greatly.'

'You're a real saint, Father.'

Quinn bowed his head. He turned over his hands and stared into the palms as though he was holding something. 'I realised I was getting in deep but I reckoned they wouldn't do anything to me because of what I'd done with the money. It wasn't as if I'd spent it on myself. But I couldn't handle it after a while so I confessed.'

'Who to?'

'A priest. Who else?'

'What priest?'

'My parish assistant, Donald Byrne.'

'Guilty conscience got the better of you, did it?'

'Brother Patrick will have told you about the stone he keeps beside his bed?' Fyfe nodded, thinking that he should take notes but not bothering. 'Well, if I got my hands on it I'd crack Byrne's skull wide open and scoop out his brains with a trowel.'

Fyfe prevented himself breaking into a spontaneous grin. Quinn and him were soul mates. 'You don't get on with him, then?'

Quinn lifted his head and shaped his lips into what was probably a sneer. 'I would gladly kill him with my bare hands for what he has done to me,' he said evenly.

'Doing the Devil's work, is he?' Fyfe said, using the parting phrase of Mrs McMorrow, the loyal housekeeper.

There was absolutely no reaction from Quinn. A pulse of blood on the side of his forehead made the wrinkled skin quiver. His tongue poked at the corner of his mouth. Otherwise there was no movement, no real expression. His ear lobes, if anything, went a deeper shade of pink but Fyfe decided that was just his own imagination working overtime. The same imagination that sensed the temperature in the room falling dramatically. Or maybe that was true because Quinn seemed to notice it as well and began rubbing his upper arms vigorously.

'Do you know about Brother Patrick?' Quinn said, leaning forward and speaking in a whisper. 'Used to be a high-flying executive in a big company. Ten years ago he started drinking heavily, left his wife and family, used prostitutes, embezzled cash to maintain his lifestyle. Went to prison. Ended up a monk here in the back of beyond, running a funny farm for burned-out priests like me.'

'Good for him.'

'Do you know what you'll be doing in ten years' time, Chief Inspector? Do you know where you'll be?'

'I don't know where I'm going to be tonight,' Fyfe replied, deciding on the spur of the moment that he would go round and visit Sylvia. He sneaked a look at his watch to check the time.

Quinn turned his head to look at the sea. He sighed deeply and his whole body shuddered. He began to run the tips of his fingers over his eyebrows. He spoke towards the window.

'My confessor was of a like mind to me,' he explained. 'When I told him what I was doing and showed him how simple it was he had this sudden vision of building an orphanage in Eastern Europe, Rumania or Albania, somewhere like that. It came to him in a blinding flash, he claimed. God had given him, given us, this opportunity to do some real good. Not just to take a bunch of kids on holiday whose idea of deprivation is a second-hand bike instead of a new one. No, this was a chance to change lives for the better, to make a real impact, banish misery, bring joy.'

'Like I said, Father. You're a pair of real saints.'

'Sounds daft, doesn't it? But I believed in it at the time. I really did. I wanted to believe in it, needed to believe in it. So we went into partnership. We siphoned off more money than ever because we thought we could put it to better use than the Church.'

'You and Father Byrne together?'

'We bought shares,' Quinn said, ignoring the question. 'If capitalists can make themselves rich, why couldn't we achieve the same result for the poor?'

'Fancy chess sets too. And jewellery. How did they square with your principles?'

Quinn shook his head. 'That was Byrne. He moved into property speculation. It is easy enough. You just set up a trust, call it after Saint Thingummyjig, and nobody is any the wiser. There are literally thousands of genuine trusts doing all kind of good all over the place. Cuckoos in the nest are not instantly recognisable.'

'It couldn't last.'

'It didn't. The cuckoo grew too big. I could lose a few thousand pounds in the diocesan books, no problem, but a few hundred thousand pounds was a different story. It was only a matter of time before we were caught. I told him that but he wouldn't stop. Didn't seem to want to stop. He enjoyed it, the risk. He thrived on it. He was in charge by then. I was too far gone. I just signed whatever he put in front of me.'

'What do you mean?'

The drink got to me. I could have as much as I liked, and I did. A bottle of whisky a night, more. Money no object, of course, and good malts too, none of the cheap stuff. I was in an alcoholic haze for six months at least.'

'Why didn't you tell somebody else?'

Quinn's hands were on his knees once more, fingers kneading at the bones. His eyes were tightly closed as if he was in great pain. 'Only a matter of time,' he said, repeating it over and over. 'Only a matter of time.'

'Time's up.'

'It was when that bloke Barrie started calling in his debts that it all began to fall apart.'

'Barrie?'

'Yeah. Gus Barrie. You must know about him. He is a drug dealer, gun runner, dodgy businessman. You name it, he's into it. He needed liquidity in a hurry for reasons I never understood.'

Fyfe knew of Barrie, a big-time crook with a snow-white record. He had questioned him several times on different investigations. Once it had been at his offices and once at his home, a Roman-style villa in dubious taste behind high walls and electronic security gates. Each time it had been a dead end. Barrie was untouchable. He remembered the Windfall Construction notice on the scaffolding at the church. That was one of Barrie's companies.

Quinn opened his eyes. 'Suddenly guys with tattoos and shaven heads were knocking on the door. We had to find money fast or we were dead. That was when the house of cards came tumbling down.'

Another silence danced slowly around them, as complete as Brother Patrick's Reebok-cushioned footsteps.

'Three weeks ago they came to get me,' Quinn said. 'I was drunk, naturally, and made a fool of myself trying to put the blame on Byrne. He had got his retaliation in first by shopping me. I wouldn't have believed me in the state I was in. He was able to play the injured innocent. They sent me here to dry out.'

'That's your story?'

'It's the truth as far as anything is the truth.'

'Suppose I tell you your Archbishop doesn't believe you. He thinks you're just a bad example for poor innocent Father Byrne. You're the criminal. Why do you want to drag others down with you?'

'There is plenty of scope for thinking here,' Quinn said. 'High cliffs and few distractions.'

'Is that all you do, think?'

'Think and pray. Prayer makes the Christian's armour bright and Satan trembles when he sees the weakest saint upon his knees.'

'Very probably.' Fyfe wondered if Satan might not be trembling with laughter but didn't say it. 'You still think of yourself as a Christian, then?'

'Yes, despite everything. I have repented for my sins. I am on my knees. I pray for Father Byrne.'

Fyfe had a hip-flask of whisky in the inside pocket of his jacket. He wondered fleetingly if he should offer Quinn a drink to see if he would take it. No. He rejected the idea and sneaked another surreptitious glance at his watch. Plenty of time yet.

'Have you met Father Byrne?' Quinn asked, changing his mood and his demeanour with a tilt of his head.

'Briefly. He was too busy to talk. I'm seeing him tomorrow morning.'

Quinn nodded and cupped his hands over his face. If he was to be believed, the old man's story would not be good news for the Archbishop. If true, it meant two rotten priests instead of one. It meant complications and huge potential for embarrassing publicity. Wonderful stuff.

'Tell me about Byrne,' Fyfe said.

'He is a renegade,' Quinn said fiercely but dispassionately. 'An apostate. A fornicator. A manipulator. A deceiver. A liar. An amoral criminal.'

'Just a regular kind of guy really.'

Quinn looked up from his hands. The profile position with the hands together in front of his face reminded Fyfe of a religious painting by some Old Master he must have seen before but couldn't put a name to. Quinn's forehead twitched erratically as though something was under the skin trying to fight its way out.

'How does a guy like that get to be a priest?'

'He wasn't always like that. People change.'

'Big change.'

'You're not a religious man at all, are you, Chief Inspector? You won't understand that just as people like Brother Patrick can be born again, so people like Father Byrne can be sucked over to the other side.'

'One sees the light while the other gets lost in the dark.'

'You have it,' Quinn said, covering his face once more. 'As you have mentioned already, it is the Devil's work.'

'You mean he is possessed by an evil spirit?'

'In a manner of speaking. But not one that jumps out at you with horns and a forked tail spitting green bile.'

'Pity. We could have charged the little devil as well.'

Quinn dropped his hands into his lap and his head sagged low. 'I deserve your mockery, Chief Inspector. But Father Byrne deserves your professional attention as a policeman. He is plausible, persuasive and well regarded within the Church. He will continue to do untold damage until he is stopped. His one weakness is that he knows he will ultimately be stopped because his empire is built on sand.'

'Only a matter of time, eh?'

'Yes indeed.'

The window rattled in a gust of wind, making them both look across. A black-headed seagull glided past on outstretched wings spiralling down towards the harbour. Its body was magnified and distorted momentarily as it passed behind a flaw in the glass. Darkness was spreading inwards from the horizon like a dust storm.

Fyfe felt sorry for the old man seated at the table beside him. He was inclined to believe his story but worried that Quinn was too plausible and too persuasive for his own good. He admitted fiddling the books to begin with and then claimed Byrne had taken over. A classic case of shifting personal blame and copping out of responsibility. The reason why Fyfe sympathised with him was because of his instinctive prejudice against Father Byrne after their brief encounter. It would be interesting to see what the younger guy had to say for himself tomorrow.

Fyfe stood up. 'This is just a preliminary meeting. I will need a full statement, including details of all your business transactions and a log of where the money went.'

'I'll tell you all I know. But I don't know what happened to most of the money. I was too drunk to realise what I was doing.'

'I thought you said you were the financial brains.'

'Byrne was a quick learner.'

'I see.' It was a reasonable scenario, Fyfe thought. So was protection of a fat bank account to provide for a comfortable, if conscience-stricken, old age. 'I'll come back next week and we'll get it down on paper.'

'I'm not going anywhere. High cliffs and few distractions.'

Quinn got to his feet, straightening slowly so that he seemed to be creaking like the floorboards supporting his weight. He shuffled away out of the room muttering to himself. Brother Patrick replaced him, arms still folded inside the sleeves of his habit, limping even more noticeably on the thick soles of his Reeboks.

'Would you like something to eat before you leave, Chief Inspector?'

'No, thank you. I have to get back. Urgent business.'

'Of course. I hope you found Father Byrne co-operative. He seemed to be in a more positive mood today.'

'He gets depressed, does he?'

'We watch him closely.'

'He told me something about you. Do you mind if I ask you if it is true or not?'

'Ask away.'

'He said you were a reformed alcoholic, a divorcee, a swindler, and a jailbird. Recognise yourself?'

'Definitely, Chief Inspector,' the monk replied with a placid smile. 'In a former life, of course.'

'That's one up for Father Quinn's veracity, then. Maybe the rest will check out as well. What do you think?'

'I do not judge, Chief Inspector. I serve as best I can.'

Fyfe sighed but concealed it behind a cough. It was the smug meekness of the clergy that annoyed him; the air of inevitability they projected that one day all unbelievers would be gathered inside the safe fold of their certainties. Maybe it would happen, Fyfe thought. Maybe one day he would see the light. Then again, maybe one day he would be sucked down into the dark. If he wasn't there already.

Brother Patrick accompanied Fyfe back to his car and stood on the steps under the row of grinning gargoyles to watch him drive away. The light was draining away fast. Darkness was accumulating on the horizon like an army gathering. The house dipped out of sight as the car made slow progress over the rocky track back towards the main road. Fyfe took the hip-flask from his pocket and held it between his knees while he unscrewed the top. He lifted it to his mouth just as the front tyre lurched into a deep pot-hole and the flask bumped painfully against his teeth. Blood mixed with the whisky as it flowed smoothly down his throat.

23

John Adamson entered the familiar flat Father Byrne had arranged for him to have on his release from prison. He had been there before but only as a visitor. Now that he was free and possessed the key it somehow looked different. It was tiny, a bed-sit room with shower and toilet and a Toytown kitchen squeezed into what had once been a cupboard. After nine years in a succession of bare prison cells it seemed ridiculously spacious. And there were no bars on the window. He pressed his fingers against the fragile glass and ran them over the flaking white paint on the frame. Above his head a corner of the ceiling paper was hanging loose and the floor was covered with three scraps of different coloured carpet. The bed had a black iron frame and a soft mattress on top of creaking springs. There was a badly put together flatpack wardrobe and a dark wood table with a straight-backed pine chair. A gas fire occupied the tiled grate where a fireplace had once been set into the wall. It was burning with a dark red flame and the air was dry and warm. The television was a small black portable.

Adamson sat down on the leather padded reclining chair and surveyed his domain. The alcohol he had consumed in a pub he had found had made him very drunk and sleepy. Over a period of two hours he had downed beer and then vodka and then, as a special treat for his first day of freedom, a speciality cocktail, called a Mindbender. He had sat in a corner for a few hours, initially worried that everybody was watching him but ultimately not caring. When he staggered out, bouncing off the walls, he was sick on the pavement but still smart enough to keep moving. He had no idea how he managed to find his way back to the flat. Suddenly, it seemed, he was at the top of the stairs fumbling with the key. Then he was inside, remembering too late to lock the door behind him before he collapsed into the chair.

He pushed back so that the support panel for his legs extended and he was able to lie back at a comfortable angle. An image projected itself on to his closed eyelids. It was of his mother's cloudy eyes lighting up when he had shared the secret of the money with her. It was his money, he had whispered to her. He had earned it and was dreaming daily of what he might do with it. She had died happy and contented, dreaming dreams of immense wealth for her only son.

Adamson could see what the oily Father Byrne was trying to do to him. Here is this person just out of prison after nine years with a secret that he thinks is his alone. Before he gets the chance to breathe deeply of the heady air of freedom he is to be hit with the revelation that the secret, or at least part of it, is shared. Shock tactics. Disorientation. Get to him before he has a chance to settle to his new life. Exploit his lack of self-confidence. Offer yourself as a solution to all his problems, a steady guiding hand in an unfamiliar world. Most of all show yourself to be on his side. Be his friend. Be a pal.

'Suppose I tell you there is no money,' Adamson said to himself, still lying back, still with his eyes closed.

'I know there is money. Your mother did not lie. You would never lie to your mother.'

Adamson jerked into an upright position. Byrne was standing over him. It was a few seconds before he recognised him in his hooded track suit. In the doorway behind was an attractive redhead with eyes blinking like camera shutters.

'I'm a priest,' Byrne continued. 'I know when people are lying. A little horned devil sits on their shoulder and whispers to them what to say. I have to cast out such devils.'

Adamson instinctively glanced at his shoulder. 'I wouldn't lie to you, Donald,' he said, beginning to enjoy himself. 'Who's your friend?'

'That's Lillian. She lives in the flat opposite. You'll get to meet her soon. Once we've got our business out of the way.'

Lillian smiled over at him. A smile as cold as frost-hardened earth on a winter's morning. Then she stuck her tongue out at the back of Byrne's head and Adamson laughed.

'You made me a promise, Jad,' Byrne said, sniffing at the obvious smell of alcohol. 'I've given you plenty of time. Forget the bloke Fyfe and the police. It's just you and me in this. It's time to deliver.'

'Okay, it's a fair cop,' Adamson said.

Byrne grinned hugely. His eyes flashed in victory. Adamson smiled over his shoulder at Lillian. He could see the priest thinking that his strategy had worked. The tactics had been right. The unsure, vulnerable ex-prisoner emerging blinking into brightly lit society had succumbed to the psychological pressure as predicted. There had been a little blip when the unanticipated appearance of a police bogeyman had interfered with the plan. But now everything was all right. The ex-prisoner had been granted his blow-out. He was drunk and easily handled once more. He was not to be given the opportunity of any more time to think.

'Where is it, then?' Byrne asked.

Adamson climbed out of the horizontal chair and got to his feet, swaying unsteadily. He didn't need any more time to think. He had decided what he was going to do. He winked at Lillian and put an arm round Byrne's shoulders. Byrne was trying it on, trying to re-establish moral control over his subject. Not a hope, Adamson decided. Not a hope this side of hell.

'I'll show you,' he said. 'Follow me.'

24

Sandy Jones huddled miserably in the entrance to the tenement close opposite Adamson's flat. He was soaked to the skin and shivering uncontrollably. When he had called his brother from the phone box on the corner his voice had almost gone. He could only speak in a kind of croaking whisper. He had to squeeze into the narrow space between the pavement and the door to avoid the run-off from the lintel. At least the rain had all but stopped. His nose was running. His head was sore. He ached all over. He was not a happy man but he did manage a fleeting smile when Billy arrived in the van, drawing up alongside him with the iron-rough rumble of worn brake pads.

Sandy knew now that he should have gone into the pub that Adamson had chosen for his binge. But he hadn't. There was no reason to keep out of his sight because he did not know him personally. He could have been warm and dry and had a few reviving drinks himself. Instead he had opted to stay outside. He had marched up and down in the rain, hiding under shop canopies and in damp doorways for two hours until it grew dark and the bastard came out and puked over his shoes. Sandy could have taken him then when he was pissed out of his head and didn't know where he was. But Billy had told him not to do anything without permission so he waited, wiping his nose with the back of his hand at regular intervals, and keeping a safe distance between them as Adamson took his erratic zigzag route. He followed him into the tenement and up the stairs and watched him unlock the door and disappear inside.

'Top flat,' Sandy said from the relative comfort of the van's passenger seat. His voice had a throaty echo to it like a badly tuned radio channel. 'Over there. The one with the light on.'

'Which one?' Billy asked.

'That one,' Sandy said with a sneeze and nod of his head, reluctant to take his hands out of his pockets until he had thawed out a bit. 'Oh no. There he is there, coming out the close.'

'Who's the guy in the jogging suit?'

'Never seen him before. They're not going jogging anyway. Look, they're getting into that car.'

'Just as well I turned up, isn't it, brother?' Billy said. 'Otherwise you would have been chasing after them on foot. They can't get away now.'

25

Fyfe killed time over a couple of pints in a basement pub not far from Sylvia's house trying to build up courage to go round and see her. His back was stiff and sore after the long drive from Tayside. He was over the limit for driving. He had phoned Catriona and asked her to keep the dogs for the night. He intended to stay in the empty flat from which his ungrateful tenants had done a moonlight flit.

He had put Father Quinn and Brother Patrick out of his mind as best he could. He had read the evening paper and knew that the double murder involved Georgie Boy Craig and his boyfriend, Michael Ellis. The other murder victim was Ross Sorley, a former associate of Craig's. They were well-known criminals and druggies. All three had been garrotted in clinical fashion. All police leave had been cancelled, the paper claimed, but when Fyfe phoned in to the office he was told he had been allocated a shift from early on Friday morning when they would begin working their way through the usual lists of suspects and no-hopers. There was no real hurry. It was an internal argument amongst gangsters. With any luck a few more would end up with their throats sliced open. The risk to the public was minimal, however big the screaming headlines were written. Even so, the Catholic Church's financial troubles and its priests' moral failings would have to wait for another day. He called home to his answering machine but there were no messages on it. Until the next morning he was off duty and free to do as he pleased.

On the pavement outside pairs of legs, cut off at waist level, walked past the window across the back-to-front gold lettering on the glass. One female pair stretching down from a short skirt stopped and turned inwards to the window. For a moment they were motionless and every fold round the knees, every tuck of skin, every smooth curve at thigh and calf with backlit downy hair was caught in sharp focus against the fluorescent background blur of the street lights. Then the legs moved, turning to go back the way they had come, walking out of the narrow frame as others walked into it; legs in trousers, legs below heavy coats, legs with bags bumping against them, and legs with thin billowing dresses wrapped round them.

Fyfe looked away, draining his glass and signalling to the barman to get him another. Sylvia had fine legs, long and straight. Sitting there on the bar stool he could feel them tightening round him as they had used to do. It was a pleasant thought and it sent a little tremor of desire through him. Down boy, he told himself. It's all in the past. No going back now. Except, he was about to go back.

He and Sylvia had drifted apart when their love affair ended. All passion was spent, neglecting their own firm insistences that they would remain friends. Initially they had met for the occasional drink but it was difficult to make small talk when there was so much between them that had suddenly become taboo. Even so he considered it a great shame when the meetings grew less and less frequent, fading into nothingness and leaving Fyfe only with a lasting memory that hung around like the smile on the face of the Cheshire Cat. Sylvia still made regular appearances in his dreams even though he was sleeping alongside his ex-wife Sally again. It was so convenient that, just as Sylvia renewed contact, Sally snapped out of her long depression and went off on holiday, leaving him on his own. Fortuitous it was. Circumstances conspiring to throw them together again. Mrs McMorrow would call it the Devil's work. It made him nervous.

He had no idea what Sylvia was playing at, agreeing to marry an old relic like Greenmantle. And why she should want Fyfe at the party was a complete mystery. To rub his nose in it? He was fascinated to find out but he wanted to get to her without being trapped inside the artificial social restrictions of party-going. He wanted to have her to himself. He didn't have the nerve to confront her sober but with his inhibitions suitably drowned he would be able to reminisce about old times. He would pretend he was seeing her to apologise for not being able to attend her party. Insincerity was a necessary by-product of the kind of civilised behaviour that was being demanded of him.

The pub was busy, he suddenly realised. People were crowding the bar on either side of him. Rock music thumped over a chorus of competing voices. The view out the window to the pavement was blocked by a roofscape of heads. He had stayed much longer, drunk much more than he had intended. Story of his life.

He thought briefly about collecting the dogs and heading home to the Borders where he could pull the covers over his head and wait for the morning. But he knew he would kick himself if he didn't make use of the

God-given opportunity to speak to Sylvia. He couldn't ignore it. If she wasn't there, at least he had tried. If she was there he might claim he had been obliged to work late. Plenty of murders around to back that one up. Maybe she would offer him a bed for the night. Why not? Old times. Old friends. Old habits.

He finished his pint and began threading his way through the crowd to the exit. Sylvia wanted to see him so he would go. It was a power she exercised over him. He did not resent it. In fact, he rather enjoyed it.

26

Father Donald Byrne parked his car as directed in a dark, tenement-lined cul-de-sac at the rear of the Palace of Holyroodhouse. Raindrop tracks scored the windscreen. The engine ticked loudly as it cooled.

'Well?' he said pointedly when Adamson made no move in the passenger seat. 'What now?'

'Follow me.'

They walked along the path into the park, sheltered by the eight-foot-high wall marking the boundary of the palace grounds. Their shadows overtook and fell back behind as they passed underneath the street lamps, seemingly floating in the air rather than being flat on the ground.

'Is this a joke?' Byrne demanded.

Adamson did not stop. His head was clear. He was no longer befuddled by drink. He knew where he was going and what he was going to do.

'You wanted me to take you to the money. I'm taking you.'

'You mean it's here in Holyrood Park?'

'Right under everybody's nose these last nine years.'

'But that's silly. Surely somebody would have found it by now.'

'Only if they dug it up and not many people dig holes in the park. The local bobbies don't like it.'

'Whereabouts is it?' Byrne asked, a lowering of his voice indicating that he was persuaded.

'On top of Salisbury Crags. A secret hiding place with a view.'

Beyond the reach of the lamps the park was intensely black. The high dome of Arthur's Seat at the centre of the park was invisible under the grey clouds covering the sky. The bulk of the nearby crags loomed menacingly in the darkness. The two men crossed the main road through the park and found the beginning of the path. There was not a car in sight.

The steepness of the slope slowed Adamson and shortened his stride. He began to breathe more quickly, feeling his legs tire as his feet slipped on the slick, smoothly worn grass of the path. A cold sweat oozed out between his skin and his clothes making him physically uncomfortable. The rain had stopped falling, but the wind still had wetness in its blustery gusts. He knew he had to hurry, had to get it over with, but he held back so that Byrne was never behind him. He never once let him out of his sight.

Byrne was very fit, looking the part of the athlete in his hooded track suit. The slope had no noticeable effect on him.

'It's not far now,' Adamson said, fighting for breath.

It took ten minutes for them to reach the highest point of the crags, where the ancient volcanic eruption had made the ground split apart and created a perpendicular cliff four hundred feet high. Almost directly opposite was Calton Hill, equally swathed in black velvet night, with the city lights spreading out around it in every direction. Ripples from a giant stone tossed into its centre.

'I sometimes come jogging along this path,' Byrne said, waiting for Adamson to catch up. 'Where is the money? Show me.'

'Near the edge.' He pointed. 'The flat stone there.'

'Right under my feet. Well, what do you know?'

Adamson had regained his breath. He had only killed once before and it had not been too difficult. Mad Mike Barrie had paid him to do it, provided the knife and everything. All he had to do was follow this old guy when he left a pub and stab him. The victim was an evil-looking bastard with a scar running down the side of his face. It ran through his eye like thread through the eye of a needle. But he died easily enough. No one had ever suspected Adamson. No reason to. It was the perfect crime.

Adamson's body itched all over. He watched as Byrne moved carefully towards the edge and leaned over to examine the rocks embedded in the ground. The ground was soft and muddy.

'Which one?' Byrne asked over his shoulder. 'This one?'

'No. The one right at the edge where no one would dream of trying to shift it.'

Byrne shuffled forward on his haunches. 'Method in your madness, Jad my boy,' he said. 'I can see that now. Is it this one?'

Adamson went over to where Byrne was crouching. He raised his leg and placed the sole of his foot on the small of Byrne's back. With the gentlest of kicks he toppled him over the edge. There was no scream, just a silent disappearance into the darkness and from below a dull thump as bone connected with rock.

'Don't worry, Father Donald,' Adamson whispered into the night, feeling the words lifted from his lips by the breeze. 'Don't worry. It's not so hard to die.'

27

Sandy Jones had to sneeze. He clamped his hand over his nose and deadened the sound as best he could. When he looked up the wind blew pinpricks of rain into his eyes. There was only one silhouette on the crags, a smear of dark grey against the only slightly lighter background. He recognised Adamson from the outline. He was standing motionless. The other one, the priest, had vanished.

Sandy was lying on the sloping ground behind the crags in the soaking wet long grass. His damp clothes were like another person clinging to his back. He was watching the scene more than fifty yards ahead of him. His nose was running. He could not feel his fingers or toes and he was shivering uncontrollably as he silently cursed his brother Billy sitting in the warmth of the van. 'You follow them,' Billy had said. 'I'll stay here in case they come back to the car.' There was a brief, whispered argument but Sandy was already resigned to being the loser. There was no time to waste. He had to keep Adamson and the priest in sight. So he went out into the cold and wet and hurried after them into the darkness.

He had to sneeze again. He muffled the outward noise but it made his head buzz inside. When he looked up Adamson was moving downhill, a shadow sliding across the dark. He had no time to think, no time to worry what had happened to the priest other than a vague idea that he might have gone over the edge. He had to keep up with Adamson.

Sandy hauled himself to his feet and, still crouching down, began to run after him.

28

David Fyfe rang the bell of Sylvia's flat and heard it jangle tinnily in the distance beyond the huge black door. The front windows were in darkness. The walk from the pub in the cold air had more or less sobered him up. If he was lucky Sylvia would be out and he would be able to turn round and go away. That would be the best thing. Otherwise he would just make a fool of himself trying to tell her she was doing the wrong thing. This way at least he would have tried to speak to her. He would have made the effort. Honour would be satisfied.

But she was in. Light suddenly leaked from under the door, making the toes of his shoes gleam. He heard the sound of footsteps and the lock turning loudly. He was confused to be confronted by an old man with a shock of silver hair. He was wearing tweed trousers and an open-neck shirt. He was holding a brandy goblet and had a fat cigar in the corner of his mouth. The upward trail of smoke from the cigar forced him to have one eye shut. He peered at Fyfe curiously from the other.

'I'm sorry,' Fyfe said. 'I thought this was Sylvia Cranston's address.'

'It is,' the old man replied. 'She's just popped round to the shops. She'll be back in a second.'

'Ah. Right.'

Realisation began to dawn on Fyfe. He took a step backwards. Without his judge's wig and robes Lord Greenmantle looked like a pensioner exhausted from a session on his allotment.

'Any message?'

'I was just calling round to... Sylvia had invited my wife and myself to her engagement party tomorrow night. I was just passing by and I thought I would make my apologies. We can't make it.'

'And you are?'

'David Fyfe.'

'Ah. Right.' Greenmantle straightened and took the cigar from his mouth. He stared at Fyfe unblinkingly from two bright eyes before transferring his glass to the cigar hand and holding out the other in welcome. 'Good to meet you. I have, as they say, heard a lot about you.'

Fyfe shook hands. 'Nothing bad, I hope.'

'Badness is relative. But no, nothing bad. Come in and wait. Sylvia will be back soon. I'll get you a drink.'

Fyfe was trapped. He could have made his excuses and left but that would have been impolite and, anyway, he was fascinated to find out what this old man had to say for himself. He shuffled nervously, unsure of how to act, asking himself once more what he thought he was doing there. Greenmantle seemed pleasant, wise even. His handshake was firm. His bony hand had freckles the size of five-pence coins on it but he was not the shrivelled bad-tempered old husk Fyfe had somehow expected. That made it even worse that Sylvia was going to marry him.

Greenmantle led him through to the back sitting-room. Fyfe knew the layout of the flat intimately. He and Sylvia had made love in every room at one time or another. Regularly they had lain naked in front of the real coal fire where Greenmantle was poking a long spill so that he could relight his cigar with much puffing and exhalation of smoke.

'You've known Sylvia quite a long time,' he said. It was not a question so Fyfe didn't bother to answer. He sat down in one of the wing armchairs as directed. 'Of course, I've known her even longer.'

The remark roused a spasm of jealousy in Fyfe. Irrational possessiveness was one of his bad failings. When Greenmantle asked what he wanted to drink he named twelve-year-old oak cask Glenfarclas because he knew it was Sylvia's favourite and she always kept a bottle handy. The old man knew about their affair. It had been no secret.

'A good choice,' Greenmantle said. 'I would love to join you but I'm afraid I cannot. This isn't brandy, you see, but warm water with a little brown paste stuff my doctor prescribes. It is the most my digestive system can cope with. I like to pretend it's brandy though. Makes me feel healthier. No harm in it, just as there is none in the water. I shouldn't smoke either, but what the hell.'

'Appearances can be deceptive,' Fyfe said, taking the whisky he was offered.

Greenmantle sat in the identical armchair on the opposite side of the fire and rested his ankles on the brass fender. 'Yes, they can, David. Inspector is it?'

'Detective Chief Inspector.'

'DCI, of course. You have given evidence in my court before now. Catch any criminals today?'

'Not a one.'

'Never mind. There are plenty out there and you've always got tomorrow.'

He must know about me and Sylvia, Fyfe decided, wondering what exactly Sylvia had told him. He shifted uncomfortably in his seat, regretting being alone with the old man, wishing Sylvia would come back. He drank whisky and avoided eye contact.

'Thank you for being a friend to Sylvia,' Greenmantle said.

'That's okay,' Fyfe replied, hugely embarrassed.

The curtains were open on the window that looked out on to the back gardens. In front of it was a chest of drawers with an antique willow pattern bowl and jug washing kit on top. It had used to be in the bedroom. The jug's pouring lip was badly cracked and stuck together after being knocked over during one energetic afternoon of run and chase sex. Behind the jug Fyfe and Greenmantle were reflected in the dark, star-speckled glass. The fire between them was a mass of writhing red. Greenmantle blew a perfect smoke ring and spoke.

'Isn't it fascinating to think that as we sit here crimes are being committed out there at this very moment which shall be the subject of proceedings in court in due course?'

'Yes. Life goes on,' Fyfe said.

Greenmantle waved his cigar at the window. 'All sorts of things are happening out there; deliberate, accidental, circumstantial. The wonder is that we ever make sense of all the chaos.'

'We don't make sense of it. At least I've never managed to.'

'You arrest them and I send them down.'

'A simple system.'

'I worry sometimes that I am going soft in my old age. Do you remember the Mike Barrie case? It's a long time ago now.'

Fyfe remembered. This was decent man-to-man talk he could cope with. He had good reasons to remember the Barrie case. Reasons that neither Greenmantle nor Sylvia could be aware of. Real secrets he had never shared.

'I remember it well,' he said. 'Mad Mike Barrie held up a security van taking old banknotes to be destroyed. The incinerator had been out of commission for several weeks for repairs and the van contained three times the normal amount of cash, well over one million pounds. They got away with the money but were trapped the next day in a flat at the East End and Mike topped himself rather than surrender. He burned the cash too so nobody else could get it.'

'You were involved in the case?'

'I was a sergeant at the time. I attended the siege and the subsequent questioning. I had to break the news to Mike Barrie's widow.'

Angela. A beautiful woman of his own age, all legs and backside, big breasts and pouting lips. She had tried to act the hard-faced bitch but that didn't last long and she had collapsed into his arms weeping inconsolably for fully half an hour. He couldn't do anything with weeping women. He just held her tight and waited for her to come round. After that they discovered an affinity for each other. It was a time when he was drinking too much, working too little, beating up suspects, using dodgy evidence, generally not caring what happened to him. The affair with Angela was passionate, very, very physical, and short-lived. It lasted ten days. He had never told anyone. He drank whisky to hide his smile.

'What a hero Barrie was,' Greenmantle said. 'A criminal martyr was created in that hour for a new generation to identify with. Do you believe the money was burned?'

'We never found it. Just a pile of ashes. Some money had been burned.'

'What about the widow?'

'We questioned her obviously,' Fyfe said, biting the inside of his lip. 'We staked her out for a while. I personally don't believe she got away with it. Of course when she decamped to the Costa del Sol there were those who said "Told you so."'

Their last night together before she flew out to Spain had been a steamy, no-chance-to-sleep session in a hotel room. If Angela had the money he would have known. They did talk about the crazy idea of him following her abroad but, despite everything, he knew the difference between fantasy and reality. Sally, still his wife at that stage, was the reality. Sylvia was a few years in the future. Angela was a present fantasy.

'Do you remember John Adamson?' Greenmantle asked.

'Barrie's sidekick? Yes. He survived the suicide with Barrie's blood all over him. You sentenced him to a fair whack.'

'Twelve years. I assumed he knew where the money was hidden and was keeping quiet so he could come back and get it afterwards.'

Fyfe shook his head. 'There was the Spanish widow route for the money and the Adamson hidey-hole route. I didn't subscribe to either. Barrie was mad and too much in charge. That money belonged to him. Adamson was a loser. Barrie didn't want anyone else getting it if he couldn't. I think he did burn it.'

'You don't think Adamson had the savvy to hoodwink his mate?'

'If he did we would have got it out of him. He had a dependent personality that was fairly easy to manipulate. His psychiatric report labelled him mildly schizoid, some psychopathic tendencies. Nothing debilitating but cracked enough to be noticeable. Trust me. The money went up in smoke.'

'Stuck to his right of silence at the trial and smirked at me when the jury returned their verdict. I added on a few years on the strength of it. I wanted to make sure he paid for the cash if he was ever going to get it.'

'I'm sure there must be plenty of legal precedents.'

'Anyway, the whole point of this story is that a couple of weeks ago a parole recommendation for Adamson landed on my desk at Parliament House. As the sentencing judge I have to approve any such recommendation and I had refused eighteen months earlier and a couple of times before that as well. Now if I had been my normal, crusty self I would have left the swine to rot for his full term. But as fickle fate would have it the previous day Sylvia had agreed to become engaged to me. Therefore, imbued with the heady spirit of human magnanimity, I duly signed the document with a flourish.'

'So Adamson is out now.'

'Yes. But if it wasn't for Sylvia he would still be inside. Random circumstance, you see, David. My favourite theory of life. Progress through random circumstance.'

'A lucky man.'

'Just like me marrying Sylvia, don't you think? That sounds like her at the door now.'

29

Still alive. Messages of pain came from every part of Byrne's body to overload his central nervous system. Intolerable. Unbearable. Inescapable. Every breath of air was like acid pouring down his throat. Nerve ends shorted against each other and made sparkling lights dance in front of his eyes. Beyond the lights he could see the grey mist and the vertical rock face and the black shapes of the long blades of grass overhanging his face. And beyond the miasma of pain he was aware that he was alive. Still alive.

Donald Byrne was lying on his back, half on the gravel roadway, half on the grass, at the foot of Salisbury Crags. He had twice hit the rock during his fall. The first contact had dislocated his shoulder. The second had smashed the left side of his skull and his right kneecap. The impact with the ground had broken his back and both legs. He could not move. He could only lie motionless, staring up at the brown rock, weathered and scored by centuries of exposure, unable to see the top of the precipice because it was lost in the luminous mist. Soundless words came from his twitching lips.

Holy Mary, Mother of God, pray for us now and at the hour of our death.

Pain screwed itself into a thumping crescendo. Then it subsided, an outgoing tide to leave him stranded on a senses-barren beach. His mind was capable of rational thought but it was trapped inside a useless, shattered body. He found the only movement he had was in the fingers of his left hand. He was just able to feel the loose gravel under the fingertips. But even moving the tiny pebbles drained him of precious energy because they seemed to be infinitely heavy.

Holy Mary, Mother of God, pray for us now and at the hour of our death.

He was terrified at the prospect of dying in a state of mortal sin, but anxious that he should die before pain overwhelmed him again. Conflicting emotions made the sky darken above him. The wind sighed mournfully through the grass around him. Blood flowed into his mouth, blocking his throat, making him cough. Blood sprayed into the air and fell back on to his face in warm, pinprick drops.

Holy Mary, Mother of God, pray for us now and at the hour of our death.

Pain walloped into him, making him quiver and groan. The sensation of feeling in his legs disappeared. He imagined they were becoming invisible, disappearing from sight. Soon his upper body and then his head would follow and he would vanish entirely. Then no one would find him. No one would know he had ever been there. He would dissolve and reappear at another place, at another time before he had ever met the sad-eyed Father Quinn and the rapacious Lillian.

How pathetic, how foolish he had been. How weak to be distracted from spiritual truth by the temptations of earthly flesh and possessions. He had no excuse to offer his maker, other than that he was a hopeless sinner like so many that had gone before him. Heaven was out of bounds. Hell would be ready for him.

Holy Mary, Mother of God, pray for us now and at the hour of our death.

The pain swarmed over him again, the sharp teeth of wild animals tearing at his bones. Blood again in his mouth, choking him, coughing wracking his body. A foretaste of hell. Of what was to come for him.

Raw fear scrabbled like horny claws tearing at his guts and made him struggle to stay alive. He spat out blood and gulped at the air. His heart beat erratically. He could only move his fingers, scratching at the gravel like a climber searching for a hold. Only his mind seemed to be in proper working order and even it was beginning to play tricks on him.

The smell of incense filled his nostrils. And he heard the rustle of stiffly starched altar robes. The chant of the Mass. Bread like paper on his tongue and sweet red wine. His mother embracing him at the ordination ceremony. His father shaking his hand. Aunt Ethel wiping away a tear. Then flame-haired Lillian in figure-hugging clothes, cloth-wrapped nipples and thighs. The smell of her, a corporeal female incense and the rustle of white cotton sheets. The wickedness and the evilly efficient lubrication of their coupling. The intensity of pleasure and the black depression of subsequent guilt before he went back for more. The vanity. The selfishness. The calculated decision to steal the Church's money while he sat in judgement of good, ordinary people who had committed the least of sins. The ingenuity he used once Quinn showed him how, the simplicity of it all. And the final desperate determination to get enough money to escape, to get out and begin a new life.

God saw everything, knew everything, accounted for everything. Despite all he had done, Byrne still retained his faith in God. It was deep and unshakeable. He believed in life after death. He believed in heaven and in hell. Oh God, how he believed.

Holy Mary, Mother of God, pray for us now and at the hour of our death.

Another surge of pain, less acute now, provoking barely a whimper. Somebody approached, looming out of the mist. An impossibly tall person, a hazy silhouette lit from behind. Unreal. Faceless. Insubstantial. A wraith. The stealer of souls come to collect a fresh one.

Byrne's fingers dug deeply into the gravel roadway. Stones shifted over them like rosary beads. He watched the silhouette grow taller, the light behind it grow brighter. Byrne gurgled on the blood in his throat and swallowed some of it. Hell was peopled by creatures such as these, he thought. Perhaps he was already dead.

Holy Mary, Mother of God. Pray for us now and at the hour of our death.

The darkness disintegrated into impenetrable black.

30

Adamson was hyper-ventilating as he ran back across the park. Headlights approached far away to his left. Red taillights glowed even further away on his right. He thought he saw somebody or something ducking behind bushes to his right. He dodged to the left and missed the path, stumbling on a steep grassy bank and plunged forward, landing awkwardly on his shoulder. He rolled over and over and kept sliding as he tried to dig his heels to stop himself. At last he did and was back on his feet running, letting the slope carry him down to the level ground. He was over the road in two strides and into the empty carpark beside Holyrood's boundary wall, restraining himself, slowing to a fast walk along the shadowed path. His shoulder ached. The hairs on the back of his neck prickled at the knowledge that behind him was the dark slab of Salisbury Crags with the dead body lying at its base.

Father Donald Byrne was dead all right. There could be no doubt about that. Adamson had crushed his skull with a handy boulder. Now his secret was safe again.

He broke into a run again, prodded by the image of the twitching body and the sickening sound of breaking bone. It had been a stupid thing to do. It confirmed a murder that would otherwise have been reasonably explained as accident or suicide. That had been his idea and it had all worked like a dream up to that point. The gentlest shove had been enough to pitch Byrne over. There had been no suspicious marks on the body apart from those caused by the fall. And then Adamson had to panic and smash his head in. No doubt then. No more twitching. Instead there was a gloriously satisfying stillness and a silence that was almost sexual in its brief intensity. He had experienced the same feeling at the moment of his first killing, when he had stabbed the old guy with the scarred face. The sensation, gone in an instant, had been more enjoyable than spending the money he was paid for the job.

'Stupid, stupid, stupid,' he muttered to himself as he ran past the car they had arrived in. The street was empty. A black and white cat stood on a window sill. It arched its back and bared its teeth as he passed.

'Stupid, stupid, stupid.'

Now there would be a murder hunt, stories in the newspapers and on television. He would undoubtedly be questioned because of his recent contact with Byrne. That would be no problem. He would stonewall them. He could manage that. He had had years of practice in prison.

Adamson moved at a brisk trot along the pavement. He had reached a busier part of the city. Other people occupied the pavements. Cars passed, sweeping their lights over him, elongating and squashing his shadow. He slowed right down to a walk and regained control over his breathing.

It wasn't so bad, he reasoned. The police would have come to question him anyway as a matter of course whatever the manner of Byrne's death. It was an obvious routine for them. In fact, that it was so clearly a murder probably worked in his favour. What would be his motive? Why should he be suspected? Why should he kill such a generous benefactor? It would make no sense to anyone unaware of the full story.

He ran through the streets when there was no one around to see him and walked when there was. He found himself standing outside the entrance door to the tenement. A tremendous sense of relief flooded through him. He had made it back. He was safe again. He could lock himself in.

31

Sylvia entered the room and stopped dead when she saw Fyfe. She had her coat over her shoulders like a cloak and Greenmantle rose in a surprisingly swift movement to relieve her of it. He disappeared through the door. She just stood there with her keys in one hand and a carton of low fat milk in the other. She was wearing high heels, black stockings and a simple black wrap-around dress with plain gold jewellery. Her hair was shorter and bleached even blonder. She seemed to be thinner than he remembered, even more attractive.

'Long time no see,' Fyfe said, standing up.

'What are you doing here?' she asked, suddenly agitated. She frowned and stepped forward to kiss him on the cheek. He felt her breasts press against his chest.

'David dropped in while he was passing,' Greenmantle said. 'He can't make it to the big occasion tomorrow night. Shame really. It's going to be quite a thrash.'

Greenmantle was buckling his thick overcoat and arranging a scarf at his neck. He pulled on a pair of gloves like a Regency dandy, ensuring that every finger was properly accommodated. Fyfe expected him to produce a top hat and silver-topped cane.

'You're not going, Graeme?' Sylvia said. 'I've got milk for the coffee now.'

'I'll leave you and David to talk over old times.' He looked directly at Fyfe and his shoulders heaved with a deep sigh. 'It's only fair since you won't get the chance tomorrow. Good to meet you, David.'

He raised one gloved hand in a curiously old-fashioned gesture, spun on his heel and was gone. Sylvia followed him to the front door. Fyfe listened to the murmur of their voices but tried not to overhear. He sat down again beside the fire and watched his reflection in the window. Sylvia joined him. Her reflection was hidden by the washing jug when she sat in the chair opposite with her knees pressed together and her hands clasped in her lap.

'It wasn't me that made him rush away, I hope?' Fyfe said.

'What do you think?'

'I have this effect on people.'

'I know.'

'So what do we do now?'

'We do what old friends do.'

'What — now? In front of the fire?'

Sylvia put her head back and laughed. The gold chain glittered and flashed at her throat. Her white skin glowed with the red cast of the fire. Fyfe drank some whisky. It was smooth and strong. It fuelled his imagination and had him pulling Sylvia down to the carpet where they tangled and rolled and made love in marvellously fluid motion. 'Your Lord Graeme won't like it,' he thought of saying. 'Lord Graeme isn't getting it,' he thought she would reply, sticking her tongue deep into his mouth to shut him up. A delicious feeling of satisfaction washed over him. They would lie together, her head on his chest.

Sylvia switched on music by reaching sideways from her chair. Violins swelled and an orchestra began to play. The speakers hung from the four corners of the ceiling like security cameras.

'You're a bastard, David. Do you know that?'

'I've heard it said.'

'You're a bastard. You should have married me. You should never have gone back to your wife. You don't hear from me for a year. Then the first thing you do is come round here intending to jump into bed with me.'

'Hang on a minute. I just came to visit.'

'Don't lie, David. I know the way your mind works.'

'Okay, I admit it. How about a quick shag for old times' sake?'

Sylvia shook her head and grinned. 'Welcome back,' she said.

'Same to you. Have you missed me?'

'No.'

'What's it all about then, Sylvia?' he asked simply. 'Why are you marrying him?'

Sylvia closed her eyes slowly and deliberately, shook her head, and opened them again. She stood up and came over to kiss his cheek and lay her head on his shoulder. When she spoke she was deadly serious.

'I want to tell you something I can't tell anyone else,' she said. 'I wouldn't be able to trust anyone else.'

'Just as well I came round, then.'

'I want to tell you why I'm marrying Graeme.'

'Go on, then. Tell me.'

'It's because he's a homosexual.'

'I beg your pardon?'

'He's gay. A raving poofter. A shirtlifter. He's not one of the blatant ones and it's not common knowledge even among his close friends, but he's as queer as they come.'

Fyfe frowned and blinked as though sand had been thrown in his eyes.

'I've known since I devilled for him and never really bothered. He was a good friend, the better for knowing he wouldn't try to slip his hand up my skirt. Now there is a purge on the judiciary to get rid of gays and he's afraid he will lose his job.'

'No one can sack a judge.'

'But they can humiliate and shame him into resigning.'

'He could always come out, announce himself publicly as the first openly homosexual judge. They wouldn't dare touch him then.'

'He can't do that. The shame would kill him. It would destroy his family. He's old-fashioned, you see. Doesn't think there is any reason to be glad to be gay. He likens it to having a drink problem.'

'From that point of view, I can understand it.'

'I thought you might.'

'So why do you have to marry him?'

'Respectability. Graeme reckons the crunch is coming within the next six months. He believes at least one of his former friends has enough of a grudge against him to do the dirty. If he is engaged to me they would be laughed at if they accused him of being gay.'

'Do you have to sleep with him?'

'Of course not. He's not interested. He's gay, remember.'

'Do you have to marry him?'

'That's another thing.' She put her forehead on his chest and took a long, deep breath. 'I won't be marrying him. We'll just be engaged for a short time. There will never be a wedding.'

'That's all right, then.'

'Yes. You see, he's got cancer. It's terminal. He might last eighteen months if he's lucky. Bladder cancer.'

'Fuck's sake. Poor Graeme doesn't have much going for him, does he?'

Fyfe tried to absorb the shock of the information about Greenmantle, tried to put it in some kind of perspective. But he couldn't really concentrate. Sylvia backed away from him. He watched her legs, imagined them tightening round his waist, her breasts hanging loose, her hands gripping him. Sweat began to gather on his face. He rolled the whisky glass between the palms of his hand.

'How could I refuse him when he asked me to become involved in this little scam?' Sylvia said with unchallengeable reasonableness. 'It will protect his name, save his family from ignominy. Really, it's not that much to ask.'

'You always were a romantic, Sylvia. Tough but tender. I hope it doesn't rebound on you.'

'It won't.'

'As long as you're sure. You won't inherit his money, then?'

'We have agreed on a suitable allocation in his will.'

'Great legal minds think alike.'

'Do you approve, then?'

'It's not up to me to approve.'

'Yes, it is. I'm asking for your approval.'

'Okay, I approve. I can think of worse things to do in aspiring for sainthood.'

'You always were very liberal in your outlook.'

'He knows, doesn't he? About you and me?' Fyfe said.

'Of course. But what I told him was that our affair had never ended, that you and I were still sleeping together once a month.'

'Why?'

'Wishful thinking?'

'What? Only once a month?'

Sylvia laughed again and sat on the arm of Fyfe's chair. She kissed the top of his head. 'I asked Graeme if I could tell you about our secret plan. I needed to tell someone as a kind of... I don't know...a kind of insurance. He said I could.'

'Very trusting of him. And then he goes and leaves the two of us alone. He probably thinks we're hard at it by now.'

'So why aren't we? It's that time of month again.'

Fyfe twisted his head round until he could look Sylvia straight in the eye. She was running her index finger gently over her bottom lip. She made no protest when he reached up to slide his hand under the cross-over front of her dress but she shied away, leaving his hand touching only air. Then she

111

moved round to stand in front of him. With a barely noticeable shake of her hips the dress fell open and slipped off her shoulders. She was wearing a skimpy bra and French knickers under a suspender belt and stockings.

'It may be a long time but I haven't forgotten your little kinks,' Sylvia said.

Her skin glowed sumptuously red in the all-enveloping firelight. The orchestral music began to race towards a climax. She was still as beautiful and desirable as ever, Fyfe thought. Maybe he should have married her when he had the chance. Too late now.

Sylvia forced one leg down either side of Fyfe in the too-cramped space of the chair. She smothered him with her body and he tasted the salty warmth of her flesh, automatically letting his hands come together in the small of her back and pulling her on.

'For old times' sake,' he said and then he could say no more because her tongue was down his throat.

32

Sandy Jones moved to a different doorway to hide from the old woman who was watching him from the corner of her ground-floor window. The curtain twitched every ten seconds to reveal a wrinkled witch-like face. 'Nosy old bitch,' he muttered as he pressed himself back into the gap to hide, instantly forgetting her when the van stopped beside him. He had phoned for Billy after following Adamson through the streets back to the flat. Now after a ten-minute delay he climbed into the seductive warmth on the passenger side and grinned stupidly at his brother. His attempt at being cool ended in a tremendous sneeze that almost bounced his head off the dashboard.

'Well?' Billy demanded impatiently. 'What happened?'

'You'll never guess.'

Sandy had stopped shivering despite his damp clothes, warmed by the sight of the dead man at the foot of the crags. A new respect for his quarry had filled him when he came across the body in the grass; a track suit with a bloody thumbprint for a head. Adamson had killed the priest then. He had shoved him over the edge and run down to finish him off. This guy Adamson was premier league stuff, not the part-timer Gus Barrie had told them about. Imagine killing a priest? Sandy admired the spread of blood and the crush of bone. He took a professional interest in the murder weapon. There was an element of jealousy in his voice as he told Billy the full story. Imagine killing a priest?

Sandy had almost delayed too long at the body. When he looked up he just caught a glimpse of Adamson turning the corner round the palace wall in the distance. He was not heading back to the car but for another exit from the park. Sandy ran after him, panting loudly, managing to keep him in view, catching up as he slowed to a walk because other people were about in the streets. It was obvious where he was going and simple to stay on his trail. He had done their job for them by disposing of his priestly protector. He was alone now. Poor bastard had made himself vulnerable. Finally, they could move in and finish the job.

'Okay, let's do it,' Billy said. 'Gus is waiting to speak to Mr Adamson.'

33

Angela Simpson applied a thick layer of cherry red lipstick and blew a big kiss at her reflection in the mirror. She fluffed out her bleached blonde hair and sprayed perfume into her cleavage. She stood up and half-turned to check that her stocking seams were straight and to see the curve as she smoothed the tight-fitting short skirt over her buttocks.

'Not bad, old girl,' she told herself, patting appreciatively. 'Not bad at all considering.'

One last look in the mirror, pushing her face right up against the glass so that not even the slightest wrinkle or blemish could escape the scrutiny. There were tiny lines around her eyes and, even worse, around her mouth, noticeable despite the masking foundation powder. She dabbed at them delicately with her fingertips as if they could be wiped away. Then she stood back and sighed, smoothing her dress over her hips, and swayed from side to side on her stilettos in a deliberately exaggerated gesture.

'Not bad considering,' she said. 'From a distance anyway. It comes to us all in time.'

She had been preoccupied by the ageing process recently, searching for and finding new cracks in her face every day as the great watershed of her fortieth birthday approached. That it happened to everybody was little consolation to a woman who relied on her good looks to maintain her standard of living. She was well aware that if she faded too much her husband Terry would dump her without a second thought for something younger and more pleasing to the touch and sight. It was, after all, how she had insinuated herself into his household four years before, shoving out the previous ageing occupant to take prime position on the sun lounger at the poolside. It was a dog-eat-dog world among the chunky jewellery, expatriate society on the Costa del Sol and she was one mean bitch well practised in the art of self-preservation. Angela bared her teeth at the mirror and rubbed off the pinkish colouring from the lipstick with her little finger.

There was a knock at the door and Terry looked into the bedroom. He was over sixty with hair dyed jet black but sideburns down past his ear lobes left a statesman-like grey. Small eyes and a pointed chin completed the badger impression. His floral print shirt was open to the waist and his belly bulged over the waistband of his trousers like jelly about to spill over the edge of a mould.

'Ready yet, love?' he said. 'The gang's all here and waiting.'

'Coming.'

'Where have I heard that before?'

'When have I told the truth about it before,' she said softly so that he wouldn't be able to hear.

He moved out of sight leaving the door open. Angela walked across the room, looking back over her shoulder to see her bottom in the mirror. Four different husbands in less than ten years left her sometimes confused over what her name was, but at least it meant she always had money in her bank account and clothes on her back. Having been widowed once and divorced twice showed that she had a healthy instinct for survival that was admired among the superannuated criminals and elderly playboys who sat around under the Spanish sun like cold-blooded lizards basking on a rock. Terry was one of the former species, an ex-accountant living on the proceeds of ambitious embezzlement that had surprisingly come off. She didn't love him, didn't even like him very much, but in return for a steady income all she was expected to do was look ornamental and be good in bed, or at least make all the running, twice a week. Hardly an onerous work schedule and she used sex the way other people used credit cards. But the cracks were starting to appear and that meant the interest rates were rising too high. She suspected the next divorce might not be too far away and then she would have to start all over again in her hunt for an alternative means of support.

It was a frustrating experience being so powerless, and feeling what vestiges of power she did have wane dramatically as she grew older. Femininity was a lifelong curse. She had managed to put together a little money in a personal bank account but not nearly enough to live on in the style to which she had become addicted. Her divorce settlements had helped swell the balance but the bastards had not accumulated their cash just to squander it needlessly on getting rid of an unwanted woman. They all had pocket calculators that did magic sums. She was reasonably sure the accountant in Terry would be able to arrange it so that she did not get a penny. His other two wives had not done well by him, discovering he was prepared to lose more in legal fees than they were seeking in the first place.

However, she did have one wild card she was going to play. Gus Barrie had been pestering her, meeting her clandestinely in the Burning Sands bar down by the harbour at Estepona and taking her back to his hotel for an afternoon of distinctly old-fashioned sex. She had no ethical problem in sleeping with her brother-in-law. Mike had been dead a long time and Gus was always so embarrassingly grateful.

Good old Gus. He never gave up on trying to persuade her to join him back home. He was rich, not exactly ugly, and would make a good, relatively undemanding husband. Her problem was that she had not been back to Scotland for almost a decade and did not relish giving up the Spanish sunshine. Also, she didn't particularly like the idea of going back and reviving memories of Mike. Sometimes, in maudlin moments, she tried to imagine what might have been if he had not abandoned her. She had loved him all right, loved him to death and no one since. Definitely none since. If things had worked out she would probably still have been mistress of a white-walled Spanish villa to celebrate her birthday but there would have been children by now and a warmth and purpose in her life that were sadly lacking. They had had it all worked out so neatly all those years ago. He had promised to make her rich. Their future had been selected from an à la carte menu, but it went wrong between the ordering and the serving up. In an actual restaurant you could send it back and have it changed. You couldn't do that in the crazy-house restaurant of life. The bastards that ran it got away with murder.

She had never forgiven Mike for killing himself the way he did. Stupid bastard, flying high on drugs, a martyr to the image he had of himself as somebody who was too beautiful to grow old. She hated him for leaving her to grow old on her own.

At the Burning Sands she had been drinking dry martinis when Gus tried his latest ruse to tempt her back home. The money from the robbery, Mike's robbery, could be recovered, he claimed. Mike's partner was due out of prison soon and he knew where it was. They would follow him and relieve him of it as soon as he dug it up.

She had crossed her legs, hooking one ankle behind the other. It was a mannerism she had when she got excited but wanted to keep herself under control. She seldom thought about the million pounds plus that Mike had stolen. He had destroyed it just as he had destroyed himself. Neither could be brought back. But she was aware of the rumours that it had been a con trick. The money had not been lost at all. There were many different versions of the story but she had discounted them all, because the principal one had her as the beneficiary and she knew for a fact the inaccuracy of that one. But even though she knew the real truth, Gus's offer was persuasive. Adamson was getting out of prison and they would follow him to the cash if he did know where it was. It was simple and maybe, by some far-fetched chance, it would prove the money did still exist. Even if it didn't, a little fantasy never hurt anyone. Why not? It was a good excuse for a pilgrimage back home.

She permitted herself to enter the fantasy that afternoon with Gus, enormously tempted by the prospect of becoming a millionairess and being in total control of her own destiny. That was what Mike had promised her but for that she needed his money. Then she could tell Terry to fuck off before he got round to telling her. She would tell Gus as well, but more sympathetically. That was real power; the only sort that mattered. Until the fantasy was ruined it would pass some time as she grew steadily older.

Angela rolled the thick gold necklace at her throat between her fingers. A birthday present from Terry. Worth less than a grand. He was definitely losing interest.

Sentimental moments were few and far between for Angela. They tended to ruin her mascara and she hated to admit that any man, even a long-dead one, could make her cry. She had learned to make the best of things as they presented themselves. Now she was trying to summon up the courage to take a huge risk. She was not a risk-taker by nature but her mind was being concentrated wonderfully every time she looked in the mirror. PMT, she thought. Pre Middle-Age Tension.

Terry stood waiting for her at the end of the corridor at the top of the stair. He held out his hand and leaned forward to kiss her. She moved her head to one side so that he did not spoil her lipstick and he caught her on the cheek instead.

'You look stunning, darling,' he said, sticking his tongue in her ear in the way she loathed and sliding his hand under the hem of her skirt to snap her suspenders.

'I bet you say that to all your wives.'

They walked down the staircase, making a grand entrance into the parlour. Fifty people were milling around with wine glasses in their hands and they all looked upwards as one at the descending couple. The polished marble floor turned them upside down and dangled them in abstract limbo. Another fifty people were outside on the terrace by the swimming pool and they all began to come inside from the evening coolness. The sky beyond the terrace was a hazy azure, dotted with large fluffy white clouds like cotton wool pads for removing make-up. The hills of the Sierra de Ronda stretched into the distance and the town of Jubrique al Genalguacil was a dark patch among them. A chorus of 'Happy Birthday to You' began raggedly and then took proper shape. Angela fixed her best smile on her face and concentrated on not tripping. Fingers and hands gently stroked her arms and shoulders and back as she walked in among her friends. It reminded her of running through the washing on the back green when she was a child.

A cake in the shape of bright red Ferrari was on a table in the centre of the crowd. The number plate read: Angela 40. A white marzipan lady was in the driving seat with yellow marzipan hair and a blue marzipan scarf flowing stiffly behind her.

'That's our Angela in the driving seat,' someone said. 'Always knew she was a fast lady.'

'Born to be wild and free,' someone else said.

'Put your foot down, Angela. Show us what you are made of.'

Angela saw the cracks, like knife cuts, across the marzipan lady's face. The slash where her mouth was grinned inanely. It was a long shot going back into the fantasy zone but it was worth trying. Time was running out.

She stepped away from her husband to pick up the wide-bladed knife that had been placed beside the cake and held it out in front of her. With a horizontal flick of her wrist she decapitated the marzipan lady. The tiny head rolled on to the table-top. She snatched it up and popped it into her mouth.

Everyone thought it was a brilliant gesture. They clapped and laughed uproariously.

34

Lillian was in his chair drinking a glass of wine when Adamson burst through the door. The panic he had felt in Holyrood Park over Byrne's dead body had changed to exhilaration by the time he came running up the tenement stairs. It abruptly changed back to panic again at the sight of the redhead whose welcoming smile quickly changed to an expression of puzzlement and concern.

'What's the matter?' she asked.

Words failed him. He could only shake his head.

'What's the matter?' she repeated. 'Where is Father Byrne? Should we call him?'

'No. No.'

'What is it? What has happened?'

'No.'

'Where did you go with Father Byrne tonight?'

A shiver of redoubled panic made him tremble as if he had been punched in the face. 'Nowhere,' he said.

He turned his back on her. The empty space of the cold landing seen through the door shimmered perversely like a heat haze between him and the door to Lillian's flat. The whole building seemed unnaturally quiet and intimidating.

'Come away,' Lillian said. 'Come across to my flat. Father Byrne asked me to look after you.'

Physical exhaustion quietened Adamson as effectively as a powerful sedative. He allowed himself to be led across the landing and through to her bedroom where he was sat down on the bed. Through two doorways he could see the door of his own flat slightly open. He wanted to close it and all the doors around him, but instead he just buried his face in his hands. He didn't want to think. He didn't want to know what was happening. He wanted to be back in his little prison cell where life was simple and the only problems were the ones he created for himself inside his head.

'I need an alibi,' he said.

'What for?' Lillian asked. 'You were with Father Byrne tonight.'

'He didn't turn up.'

'But I saw you leave with him.'

Adamson felt a prickly sensation in his fingers and toes and a sudden heaviness in his stomach. Latent panic seeped into his thoughts like damp stains spreading over the surface of his brain. What was he saying? He had made another mistake. No one yet knew that the man was dead. Why should he need an alibi unless he had advance knowledge of the situation? Unless he had committed the murder?

Stupid, stupid, he muttered silently. He should have kept his mouth shut, just as he should have left Byrne to die a natural death after the fall. But he hadn't kept his mouth shut, and he had battered Byrne with the boulder.

'I'll be your alibi,' Lillian said. 'I'm an excellent liar.'

He lay back on the bed and listened to her moving about in the flat. Slowly it dawned on him that she was the only person who knew he had been with Father Byrne that night. She was the only witness who could condemn him. Logic dictated that he should kill her to protect himself. With complete objectiveness he decided he would sleep with her first and kill her in the morning.

He heard a strange sound, like something falling heavily on the floor. Strange voices. Scampering feet. Panic flapped around him like the heavy canvas walls of a tent that had been blown apart in a storm when he was a child and a member of a Scout troop on a camping weekend. The tent had collapsed on him, its rough, damp surface pressing on his face. He pushed it one way and then the other but still he could not escape. When he tried to scream it clamped itself on his lips and tried to get into his mouth. He could not breathe and he thought he was going to die. Then suddenly he was free and all the others were standing around him and over him. They were all laughing but he could not hear any sound other than the storm and the howling of the wind.

In the bedroom he sat up. His breath came in short, sharp gasps. Calm returned suddenly, just as the heavy canvas had been whisked off the terrified young Scout. But then there were more sounds and the panic came hurtling back, flapping at him as if it was descending from the ceiling. With it came a high-pitched whining inside his skull like the sound of bombs dropping. He raised his arms to protect his head from the imagined threat. Gradually the feeling subsided and he feared for his sanity. There were going to be no explosions. There were no bombs. He was safe.

Calm again, he looked up. Shock made him tremble. In front of him stood two men. They could have been mirror reflection except only one was holding Lillian by the neck. Her head was at a crazy angle on his shoulder and her feet were not touching the ground.

'Who are you?' he managed to say.

A heavy weight thumped down on Adamson's legs. Hands grabbed his upper arms, squeezing painfully. A shaven head and stubbly face appeared directly in front of him, the nose almost touching his. He couldn't move. He smelled bad breath and saw small patches of eczema peeling from raw skin round a lion's head tattoo.

'Who are you?' Adamson repeated, almost choking on the words.

'Us?' his attacker growled. 'Friend, we're your worst nightmare.'

35

A host of corpulent monks in white ankle-high Reeboks were marching past the window and Fyfe was surrounded by a crowd of stone-faced gargoyles all drinking and smoking furiously. To one side in a wing-backed leather chair sat Lord Greenmantle sucking contentedly at a fat unlit cigar. Behind him stood sad-eyed Father Quinn, Brother Patrick with his arms up opposite sleeves, and Archbishop Delaney. On the carpet at Greenmantle's feet were the Archbishop's secretary Miss Lyle, and Quinn's housekeeper Mrs McMorrow. Both of them were sitting with their legs crossed like little children and they were eating from plates piled high with sandwiches and sausage rolls. Sylvia and Sally appeared next, arm in arm, moving towards him but blithely ignoring him when he spoke their names. They did not stop, did not deviate. They walked right through him as though he did not exist and the gargoyles howled with laughter.

Fyfe woke abruptly to find a strange man's face within a few inches of his own staring straight back at him. The shock was enough to snap him into a kneeling position and that movement was enough to show him that the face was his own, reflected and distorted by a magnifying make-up mirror on the bedside table. He was suddenly aware that there was somebody behind him. He jerked away as Sylvia sat up and touched his arm with her hand. The real world re-established itself. He found his place in it and collapsed face-down on to the bed, pulling a pillow over his head.

'You always were a restless sleeper,' Sylvia said, tucking herself in closely against him. 'Something disturbing your dreams?'

He almost said, 'Something disturbing my life,' but he thought better of it. Everything he had done, they had done, over the course of the night came back to him in a rush. He smiled beneath his pillow, sighed silently and began to invent excuses that would allow him to leave at the earliest opportunity. He was wide awake, too alert to be able to return easily to the surrealistic safety of his dream. Sylvia breathed deeply and evenly beside him, creating a hot spot on his shoulder blade. He peeked out the side and blinked to clear the stickiness from his eyes. The clock told him it was only five thirty in the morning. His clothes were in an untidy heap beside the bed. His pager was fixed to the belt of his trousers. He could reach it without too much difficulty to flick the test switch. Beep, beep. Beep, beep. The noise started loudly and faded after the first couple of beeps, sounding like a bumble bee failing to get its motor running properly.

'Aw shit,' he moaned indistinctly from below the pillow.

'Shut it off, will you,' Sylvia said.

She pushed him towards the edge of the bed. He rolled off on to his feet and silenced the pager. 'I'll use the phone in the hall,' he said. 'You need your beauty sleep.'

She did not look up when he left the bedroom. He stood shivering in the hall for a couple of minutes pretending to call the office, speaking banalities to a howling telephone line that seemed to cause an echo inside his head. When he went back into the room Sylvia was still lying in the same position, her blonde hair all spiky and ruffled, the makeup round her eyes badly smudged. A tremendous wave of affection made him stand still and stare down at her. He wanted to be gone but wished he could stay. He wished he could wrap himself round her body and cling to her for ever after. What was it his mother used to tell him as a boy? You'll wish your life away.

'I've got to go, Sylvia,' he whispered, hoping she would be asleep.

She stirred, turning on to her back, stretching sinuously under the covers so that they took on the shape of her body. 'What is it?' she asked.

He had to improvise. 'Looks like another murder. Whole city's gone mad. They need me back on the bridge at the mother ship.'

She sat up and watched him dress. He couldn't think of anything witty to say so he kept quiet. The previous day had been a trying one, packed with crooked priests and ex-alcoholic monks padding about in white Reeboks. Then he had revived an old affair with his former lover Sylvia who was getting married to a queer old judge who was trying to avoid having the twilight of an otherwise blameless career on the bench blighted by the curse of arse banditry. The prospective wife-to-be had got hold of him to demonstrate her continued heterosexuality at great length.

'Once a month is it to be then, Sylvia?'

'Is that a threat or a promise?'

'A polite request.'

'What about your wife?'

Fyfe realised that Sylvia was near to tears. She was sitting with her arms folded, every muscle tensed. The bedroom looked unchanged from the time when he had been a regular visitor; the same wallpaper, the same furniture, even the same severely cut work dress hanging on the wardrobe door with her advocate's cloak draped over it. What about his wife Sally, he wondered. He wouldn't tell her what had happened, of course. He would just go back to his old habits of having both women while he could. He would burn the candle at both ends and this time when he was caught he would retire gracefully to the sanctuary in Tayside where Brother Patrick would smile indulgently and understand perfectly.

'I don't know if we should, David,' Sylvia said. 'Maybe it would be better if we just make this a one-night stand.'

He wasn't surprised or disappointed. He was aware of his dishonourable character trait of wanting to spend the rest of his life with whatever woman he happened to be sleeping with. But he was out of Sylvia's bed now, ready to move on.

'For old times' sake,' he said.

'Something like that. We might be better to let sleeping dogs lie.'

'I'll call you anyway.'

'Yes. Do.'

Fyfe bent down to kiss her on the lips. She did not resist or draw away. He could sense her eyes following him when he left and went out into the cold, clear air of the grey morning. Overnight rain had washed the streets clean. The sandstone buildings had a freshly scrubbed look about them. A milk float purred gently along the street. Two boys ran back and forward to it. Glass bottles clicked and rattled. Only when the float overtook him did Fyfe realise he was walking in a daze. He breathed deeply to fill his lungs and began heading in the direction of his car parked more than a mile away. He bought a paper from an early-opening shop and read the front page story about the three murders and the assumed gangland war. It was strong on gory description, weak on actual detail. Then he turned to the horoscopes and picked out his star sign. Love: You will renew acquaintance with an old friend. Fortune: Money is something which causes you a lot of concern.

'Right on both counts,' Fyfe said to himself.

36

Angela Simpson had Esperanza the maid drive her to the airport at Gibraltar. Esperanza was nineteen years old and not very keen on getting behind the wheel of the powerful BMW at first. She was amazed that she should be asked but, once over the shock, soon allowed herself to be persuaded. She quickly began to enjoy herself, fondling the gearstick with eager youthful fingers.

'You don't have to take the car straight back,' Angela told her when her luggage was piled high on an airport trolley. 'Go for a spin, why don't you?'

'Señora Simpson,' Esperanza gasped gratefully.

'Yes. Keep the car for the day. In fact, have the day off. Take your boyfriend out in it. Go on. Impress him. You'll have him eating out of your hand. Men can't resist beauties and this car is a beauty.'

'Señora Simpson. Thank you very much.'

Angela watched the big car move smoothly away. Esperanza was a beauty too, young and slim and dark-haired with big round eyes and the kind of eyelashes that many women would kill for. She had a fine figure and a fondness for loose-fitting dresses with low neck-lines and thin shoulder straps. God, how Angela hated her. She had never seen her boyfriend but imagined him to be a well-muscled, hairy-chested, strong-tongued Latin lover. The lucky bitch. Plenty of room for them on the back seat of the BMW to test its suspension.

Terry, Angela's husband, was playing golf. When he got back it was likely he would be drunk and would try to report a missing wife and a missing car to the police. The car, almost certainly, would cause him more concern when he found it gone. She had told him she was going to an aged aunt's funeral in Edinburgh. Auntie Mabel. An old woman. Sudden death. Totally unexpected. She had been as strong as an ox. He hadn't really been listening but that was her cover story anyway. She left a note, too, so he would remember.

Normally Angela never used the BMW. She got around in a little Renault that was all she needed. But once Terry was safely on his way to the golf course with his friends Angela loaded up the BMW with a selection of travelling cases and began her journey back to home ground. She had packed secretly the previous evening before the birthday party began, agonising over what to leave behind, leaving the half-dozen cases stacked inside her changing room. All her worldly goods. If Terry had noticed he might have wanted to know why she needed so much stuff for a weekend away. But he didn't notice so he didn't ask. After the party he had wanted sex but didn't get it. She hoped he had had all he was going to get from her.

In the morning he had been thoughtful enough to try not to disturb her when he got up early. She pretended to be asleep while he dressed, willing him to hurry up and get out of her life.

The drive along the coast road had been exhilarating on a lovely morning. Sea and sun-splashed countryside all around her and the villa getting further and further behind. No turning back now, she imagined, knowing she had set things up so she could turn back at any time. Even so, there was a little knot of tightness in her stomach that reminded her of her first day at school, and then the same feeling again when she married Mike Barrie. There were other emotions too that she kept suppressed, other memories chasing her. 'Faster,' she said to Esperanza. 'Faster.'

Angela pushed her heavily laden trolley into the terminal and found the check-in desk for the London flight. She noticed that a few men turned their heads to look at her as she passed, high heels clicking sharply on the floor tiles. The desk clerk was a young man with a large mouth and perfect teeth. His smile seemed genuine enough and she could tell he wasn't just looking at her face, but at the rest of her as well. As always, it made her feel superior.

'Can you smell it?' she asked.

'Señora?'

'My boats burning.'

'Señora?'

'Never mind. I've got a return ticket anyway. Just in case.'

37

The hood was ripped from Adamson's head and an intensely bright light shone in his eyes, forcing him to screw them tightly shut. He did not want to look, did not want to know who had kidnapped him. But he knew already and the knowledge caused huge tears of helplessness and despair to course down his cheeks.

'How are you, Jad?' Gus Barrie said.

Something sharp jabbed into Adamson's ribs, making him cry out and try to jerk his body away. The bright light had retreated enough for him to be able to see Barrie crouching directly in front. He was closing a flick-knife. The handle and the blade formed a pyramid between the palms of his hands. The knife had been used to free Adamson's arms, allowing him to sit up and scramble backwards until a corner stopped him going any further.

'Don't worry, Jad,' Barrie said. 'You were my brother's friend, I have no intention of hurting you.'

Adamson didn't believe him for a second. He pressed back into the corner, finding a curious comfort in the hardness of the walls. Dried blood was thick in his nostrils and heavy on his upper lip. Mike Barrie had been a mad bastard and his big brother was probably the same. Adamson had heard the name spoken while he lay trussed up and helpless on the floor. After hours of fearful ignorance it all began to make a horrible kind of sense when he heard Barrie's name spoken. Barrie, like the priest, thought he had kept the money. The secret that had sustained him for so long now wanted him dead.

'I don't have the money, Mr Barrie,' Adamson said. 'I just bragged about it a lot. It was good to play the big man inside. I let people think I had a secret. It made others look up to me. Sometimes I even believed it myself. But the money was destroyed, Mr Barrie. Honest, it was, the night Mike died. He made sure of that. We were both going to kill ourselves if we didn't succeed, only I didn't have the guts to go through with it. That's the honest truth, Mr Barrie. Honestly.'

Barrie held the closed knife in a fist against his cheek. The dimly lit room was full of floating dust. It was cold. The breath of the men vaporised in stringy grey clouds that floated around them like fish in an aquarium. Behind Barrie were the two muscle-men who had killed Lillian and attacked him in the bedroom, slipping the pillow case over his head, hurrying him down the stairs into the back of a van, and then into this room. He was thrown in, face down so that he cracked his nose on the hard floor and it started to bleed. A red sunrise flowered on the whiteness.

One of the heavies was holding a torch, and the other was making shadow figures of rabbits' ears in the circle the beam formed against the far wall. Adamson had been left for hours, his whole body trembling like a tuning fork because of the cold and the fear of what might happen. When he first heard Barrie's name an edited version of nine-year-old events leaped out of his memory. He could remember so much, so vividly; a scratch on the paint of the security van, the weight of the plastic bags full of money like sacks of potatoes, the desperate argument over what had gone wrong, wild-eyed Barrie booby-trapping the money, the smell of the petrol, the tiny flame and the coldness of the room, the headlong run through the streets, the curiously hollow echo of the shotgun blasts, the flower pattern of the wallpaper in the fatal flat, Mike Barrie's resigned shrug, and then his crumpled skull and the new pattern on the walls and ceiling, and the surge of policemen around him, and the dry stuffiness of the blanket over his head as they led him out, and the bright sterility of the interview room, and the challenging glare of the detective called Fyfe trying to look inside his head and discover the secret that was all he had left by then.

'I know all that, Jad,' Barrie said reasonably. 'I know what happened to the real money. I'm not accusing you of anything. I just want you to do a little job for me. That's all. Nothing too difficult. I want you to act a little part.'

'What part?'

Barrie opened his hand and rubbed a thumb along the edge of the closed knife. 'Mike's widow is coming here soon. I want you to give her the money back.'

Adamson swallowed a throatful of viscous, evil-tasting saliva. His heart started to beat very fast. The whistle of falling bombs began to impinge on the background. He touched his nose and fresh, liquid blood ran into his mouth. Barrie stood up and towered over him.

'There is no money, Mr Barrie. I've told you. It was burned. The booby trap went off and it was incinerated. It wasn't a trick. It happened. There is no money.'

'It didn't happen, Jad. Trust me.'

Panic was descending on Adamson again. The same panic he had experienced on running away from Father Byrne's body. The same that had overwhelmed him in Lillian's bedroom. He pressed back into the unyielding corner. Above them the pigeons cooed and scratched in the attic. He clasped his hands together over the top of his head. There was nothing else he could do to protect himself. The secret was killing him. He was at Barrie's mercy.

'The money exists, Jad,' Barrie said. 'Look, I'll show you.'

There was no apparent signal but the two skinheads immediately stopped their shadow game and went over to a steel chest. An open padlock was dropped to the floor with a thud. They each took one side of the lid and raised it up.

'Go on, Jad. Take a look.'

They made no attempt to hurry him. He sat in the corner for several minutes, shaking his head, refusing to move. Barrie just stared at him coldly. The two skinheads smiled inanely like game-show hostesses displaying the star prize. Eventually curiosity overcame Adamson's fear. He crawled over and peered inside the chest. There were three bulging black sacks. One was open at the top. Crisp ten-pound notes spilled from it like foam over the rim of a beer glass.

'One million, three hundred and seventy-five thousand, two hundred and forty-eight pounds,' Barrie said from behind him. 'The bank's officially recorded loss.'

'We counted more,' Adamson said.

'How many times did you count it?'

'Just the once.'

'You must have made a mistake.'

'But I was convinced the money was destroyed. The place burned down. Nobody knew it was there until I told them afterwards. They found charred notes. Ashes.'

'Keep believing that, Jad,' Barrie said. 'Mike's romantic gesture was very sincere. This is my money. I've been collecting it here for some time now. It's all used notes. Just like it should be.'

Sitting on the floor, Adamson looked from Barrie's face to the sacks of banknotes and waited for the punchline. 'Why?' he asked finally when none came.

'I told you I wanted you to act a part, Jad. I want you to take this money up to Angela, Mike's widow, and say that it is the money from the robbery. You will say you are very sorry you've kept it all this time but you didn't trust anybody enough to tell them your secret while you were in prison. That's all. Nothing more. Then you can go.'

Adamson hesitated. 'Why would I do that? Why would I give it back if I've kept it all this time?'

'Because I asked you to, Jad.' Barrie's smile grew even colder. 'Because I waited until you got out of prison. Then I had you followed to the hiding place, and then I asked you nicely to return it. If you're lucky Angela might even consider giving you a reward. In fact, I'm almost sure she will.'

Adamson backed into the corner again, pressing his fingers against the solid walls. 'But why?' he said. 'Why this charade? Why are you doing this?'

'I have my reasons. It's family business. I want Angela to believe this is Mike's money. You are the only person who can make her believe that. You're not going to disappoint me now, are you, Jad?'

'How much is the reward?'

'A very practical question. You act your part well and it will be extremely generous, I assure you. All you have to do is convince her. Can you do that?'

Adamson didn't believe him, but he needed time to think. He was beginning to have hope that he would be able to get out alive. Barrie was waiting for an answer. He had the flick-knife open. The blade was the brightest object in the room. One of the heavies was wiping his nose delicately with a handkerchief.

'I can do it,' Adamson confirmed.

'Good,' Barrie said, snapping the knife shut. 'You have made me a very happy man indeed.'

38

Fyfe headed for his office the way a ship heads for port in a storm. Grey daylight revealed a low cloud canopy and was the trigger for a renewed drizzle. His mind was operating on two levels simultaneously as he tried to rationalise his love life and suss out Father Quinn. The basement level of his subconscious was also trying to identify some pattern in the three murders that he knew would be thrust under his nose before the breakfast he still hadn't had. He had an unsettling idea there might be a connection. With Quinn, not his love life. Quinn had mentioned Gus Barrie calling in his debts. Barrie was into drugs. Three drug dealers were dead, one of them Barrie's main competition.

Fyfe drove back to Fettes, almost running into the rear ends of a couple of cars at red lights, so difficult was it for him to concentrate on real life. It had not been a good idea to rekindle the affair with Sylvia, he had decided. Not a good idea at all. Better to let sleeping dogs lie, as she had said. Which reminded him that he would have to collect his dogs sometime that day. He should have reasoned with her and talked her out of it. They could still be friends, he should have said. He could be a supportive shoulder to cry on while she indulged herself in her crazy plan to save the reputation of a gay judge. Not a lover, just a good friend. He should have told her that, he thought, shaking his head ruefully as he did so. Fat chance. He could no more resist Sylvia when the hormones were high than he could fly in the air.

He avoided the main incident room and went for a shower as soon as he got to the office. He used a discarded towel and shampoo that had been left lying around. The water was only lukewarm but it cleaned him up and made him feel better. He didn't have a change of clothes so he just had to get dressed in the same ones again. He used a finger and tap water to clean his teeth. He dried his hair and then polished his shoes with the towel. He was surprised to be buoyed up by a perverse sense of well-being and an inappropriate good humour. He checked at a mirror to see that he was inside the right body.

The incident room was sparsely populated when he finally got there just after seven. The place gave the impression of inactivity and emptiness. Bill

Matthewson came hurrying over to him as he pushed money into the coffee machine. He seemed very agitated and eager to speak.

'There's been another one.'

'Another what?'

'Another murder.'

Fyfe raised his eyebrows. The coffee machine started whirring. Another murder. That was what he had told Sylvia. Another murder. The whole city's gone mad. Maybe he was psychic?

'Is it connected?' he asked.

'We don't know yet. The body was found at the bottom of Salisbury Crags in Holyrood Park.'

'Very scenic. It's not a suicide, then?'

Matthewson shook his head. 'Skull bashed in. Bloodstained boulder left lying at the side.'

'No ritualistic throat cutting. Could be a coincidence.'

'Could be. Probably is. Different modus. Wait till you hear who it is.'

'Who?'

Fyfe picked out his cup of coffee and grimaced at the bitter taste. Matthewson stood with his arms folded, making the most of his superior knowledge. Waiting to be coaxed.

'Are you giving me three guesses?' Fyfe said. 'Who the fuck is it?'

'It's your priest.' Matthewson's mouth twitched but he managed to stop himself smiling.

'My priest?'

'That's right. Father Donald Byrne. He was found just a couple of hours ago. Still warm but definitely dead.'

Fyfe took a few seconds to absorb the news. He experienced an inner calm that allowed him to take another sip of his coffee and not notice the taste. There had to be a connection to Quinn. 'Are you sure?' he asked.

'Ninety per cent. Identification comes from a credit card in his bum bag and he also had labels with his name on sewn into his track suit.'

'The lengths people will go to just to avoid me. I was supposed to have an appointment with him this morning. I was going to postpone it. No need to now. What's happening?'

'Detective Superintendent Munro is in operational charge of the first three murders. He's taken this one on as well until we know more. He's out at the guy's church right now.'

'I was there yesterday. Should have hung around.' Fyfe drained the coffee cup. 'I'll catch up with him there.'

'The Chief is talking about you fronting a press conference with Munro this afternoon to keep the hacks happy.'

'Why me?'

'You're photogenic, apparently.'

'That's nice to know.'

Fyfe drove across the city. It was just waking up. Cars multiplied, pedestrians increased exponentially. He wondered if he was just waking up too, emerging from a strange dream that had only begun with the procession of Brother Patrick lookalikes in their white Reeboks.

He turned a corner and the sight of the ugly concrete church made him wince, as if a camera flash had gone off in his face. Father Byrne's likeness floated in front of him as he walked to the church house door and showed his identity card to the constable there. The priest had been bad-tempered, impatient, and anxious to get away the day before. Things were already happening then. Different elements were combining to produce a result. Byrne was heading irresistibly towards his death. The person waiting in the car might be implicated. Had he deliberately kept his head down to avoid being recognised? Byrne had driven him away and now Byrne was dead.

Mark Munro met Fyfe outside the study door, drawing it closed behind him. Fyfe caught a glimpse of Mrs McMorrow seated at the table with her permed Harpo Marx hair. It was easy for Fyfe to imagine her hunched over late at night sewing name tags into the good Father's underwear by lamplight.

Munro was a tall, wide-shouldered man, almost too big for the narrow corridor of the house. He was in his fifties and Fyfe knew him well from old drinking and storytelling sessions. He had a broken nose and a huge chin hanging like the pouch of a pelican's beak. He had the kind of blunt, no-nonsense approach to police work that Fyfe admired. He had been divorced twice and married three times and had an infant son a few months younger than his first grandchild. Old men will be old men, he was fond of saying.

'Anyway, I'm told you were checking this priest out for fiddling the parish expenses,' Munro said.

'Not quite as straightforward as that, I'm afraid. It was the boss priest here who is the prime suspect, fat Father Quinn. Father Byrne turned him in, shopped him to Bishop Whatsisname.'

'Delaney.'

'Yeah. Delaney wanted the investigation to be done on the quiet and our Sir Duncan used to be an altar boy or something so I was sent round to do his bidding.'

'Bloody hell, Hunky Dunky won't be able to keep it quiet now. What have you got so far?'

'It doesn't take much detective work to see that Quinn is as guilty as sin. He admits it.'

'Did you talk to Byrne?'

'Very briefly. I had arranged to interview him this morning. Looks like he is otherwise engaged.'

'Was he a crook too?'

'Well, he was a shifty-looking character and fat Father Quinn will tell you that his assistant priest was the main man in the money-embezzling racket. Who knows?'

'Was he?'

'Maybe. I didn't take to the poor bastard but that was just a first impression. Quinn hated him but that could have been his guilty conscience. The Bishop had a high opinion of him, for what that's worth.'

'Archbishop actually.'

'Does that make his opinion worth more?'

'Probably.'

'What are the chances of suicide? The crags are a favourite place.'

'Absolutely nil. Unless he smashed in his own head with a handy boulder when the fall didn't do the trick. We've got the blunt instrument. No, the scenario is he was pushed off the crags and then the murderer came down and finished him off as he lay moaning in the moonlight.'

Fyfe wondered when it had happened. Maybe while Sylvia was stripping off and climbing on top of him on the fireside chair. Maybe when they had moved through to the bedroom. 'Got a time of death?' he asked.

'Not yet. We're assuming it was around midnight.' Munro sighed deeply. 'We're not getting much sense out of the housekeeper. She's in shock. She was rambling about this guy Quinn. I couldn't work out who he was supposed to be.'

'Quinn's the boss priest. He's in a retreat up in Tayside. I was there yesterday.'

'Could it have been him?'

'No.' Fyfe said it quickly and then thought about it. 'No. He wouldn't be capable. I liked him.'

'That is hardly evidence for the defence. When did you leave him?'

'Don't know. Round about four or five.'

'So he had plenty of time to sneak down here and bump off his pal?'

'I suppose so. It never occurred to me. But I'll tell you this, Mrs McMorrow knows who did it.'

Munro was wiping his nose with the back of his hand. He stopped in mid-wipe. His large head seemed to be balanced on the axis of the flat hand under the end of his nose. Then he snorted derisively and it fell off.

'It's true,' Fyfe insisted. 'I'm surprised she hasn't told you. It was the Devil. For her, everything is the Devil's work.'

Munro snorted again and wiped his nose with his other hand. 'It will never stand up in court. By the way, Dave, you look dreadful. If you were to be found at the foot of Salisbury Crags they would think you were dead too. Didn't you sleep last night?'

'Where have you been, Mark? Looking bad like this is the latest in masculine fashion. Don't you know I'm photogenic?'

'Christ, Dave, you haven't shaved, your suit's died the death of a thousand creases, and your breath would knock over a skunk at fifty yards.'

'Just like old times, eh?' Fyfe said, putting a hand over his mouth. 'I'll go take another shower and freshen up. What are you going to do now?'

'I do have one hot tip. The housekeeper was able to tell us about a block of flats the Church runs down the bottom of Easter Road. They provide accommodation for ex-cons and reformed druggies. Anyway, she... McMan... Mc...'

'Mrs McMorrow.'

'She says the newest tenant had been with Father Byrne more or less all day since he collected him from Saughton. They had been driving around together. Byrne gave him money.'

'I wonder if he has an alibi.'

'We'll soon find out. I'm going round there now with the boys. Want to come? You've met the bloke before.'

'I have?'

'A long time ago. It took me a while to put a crime to the name but I remembered in the end. If I'm right you were in the squad that lifted him originally, Dave.'

'Who is he?'

'Think of the big security van robbery about ten years ago. More than a million quid vanished into thin air and that mad bastard Mike Barrie topped himself in a gun siege.'

Munro had his arm round Fyfe's shoulder and they were walking down the corridor. The pain in Fyfe's sore head was snuffed out, overwhelmed by the dizzying sensation of a great echoing empty space inside his skull. The connections were fitting into place. He let himself be steered towards the outside door, thinking of Lord Greenmantle's story about Adamson's parole only being granted because Sylvia had accepted his proposal of marriage.

Things were happening out there, Fyfe thought. They had been happening as he and Greenmantle had stared out the window into the darkness. Happening as he and Sylvia made love for old times' sake. Wheels within wheels. Ancient cause and delayed effect.

'John Adamson,' Fyfe replied. 'I was talking about him to a friend just last night.'

'What a coincidence. You did arrest him, didn't you?'

'Oh yes. I put him away.'

'Small world, isn't it?'

'Small city too. This is spooky. Say the name and he pops up. I can hardly believe it.'

'Well, believe it. He's back. Let's go and see what he has to say for himself.'

39

Angela Simpson caught a glimpse of central London as the plane descended through a hole in the clouds. She saw the twist of the river and church spires, and office blocks, and buildings stretching endlessly in every direction among the patchwork of green spaces all trussed up by the stringy lines of roads and streets. Puffs of cloud sped past the window, reminding her of a journey in a steam train with her father when she was a very young girl. The carriage had smelled of leather and rain-damp clothes. She was standing in her father's lap, fascinated by the vibration of the glass against her hands. When the train rounded a bend she could see the engine up ahead puffing great gouts of white smoke, and she could feel fingers burrowing in under the elastic of her knickers. The bastard, she thought, squeezing her empty plastic glass until it cracked. May he rot in hell for ever.

The plane seemed to pick up speed as it got closer to the ground. Two long-necked swans flew alongside, their wings beating in perfect synchronisation. Angela turned her head to keep them in view as the plane approached Heathrow but within seconds the beautiful white birds were too far behind. A stewardess took her cracked gin glass and the miniature bottles.

Angela had helped herself to five gins on the flight and was feeling drunkenly sleepy. She was still surprised she had actually gone through with it, still a little in shock that she had been brave enough to pack her bags and leave, even if she had bought a return ticket for insurance. For the time being at least, she was finally on her own.

She hadn't felt like this since she was a trembling fourteen-year-old, sitting on her bed, staring in awe at the door through which her father had fled, the bloodstained razor blade in her hand dripping thickly on to the sheets. Something was hardening inside her again, had been doing so for several days, as it had done before on that single night when she had somehow found the strength to liberate herself from a lifetime of abuse. It was a watershed, a point of no return, the birth of an implacable determination.

The wheels bumped on the runway, screeched and rumbled. Home at last, somebody shouted from the front like a black revivalist preacher and there was a ripple of amused cheering. But she wasn't home yet. She had to find her way across the terminal to catch the Edinburgh shuttle. Another plane, another couple of gins. She slipped a little deeper into her maudlin mood.

An hour later her home city was below, a shapeless mass of lights with the black hole of Arthur's Seat at its centre. Here she had met and married Mike Barrie and watched him die. Their wedding, a fluffy-sleeved white dress and kilt and bow-tie affair, with her father giving her away, livid white scar tissue stretching from his forehead down through an eye and the corner of his mouth, petering out on his chin. He didn't know then that he had just two weeks to live, stabbed to death in an apparently motiveless attack as he walked home from the pub. What a tragic homecoming for the young honeymooners who had enjoyed the most satisfying sex Angela had ever known that night.

She had told Mike about the years of abuse and he had arranged to have her father killed for her. Simply. Clinically. No messing. Her father deserved to die, probably wanted to die to atone for his perversion. She certainly wanted him dead. He had never interfered with her again after she slashed him with the razor blade. Nine years they had played at proper father and daughter and never once had it been mentioned. Her mother had been too stupid, too frightened, or too ashamed to acknowledge its existence. The scar was explained away as the result of random violence. Poor bastard, seemed to attract motiveless attackers.

Now it was another homecoming. Nine years she had waited patiently for her father's death and it had been nine years since Mike buried her fortune and forgot to come home to give her the treasure map. There was a pleasing symmetry in that realisation. How long had she and Mike been married? God, yes. Nine years. The bloodletting, it appeared, had its own regular pattern, a periodic one like a menstrual cycle. She hiccupped loudly and held her hand to her mouth to stop a giggle following.

The plane had landed and she had barely noticed. The passengers were standing up, collecting their belongings from the overhead lockers. Angela was thinking about the policeman informing her Mike was dead. He had been young, around the same age as her, and handsome in a hangdog sort of way. He had looked directly into her eyes and she had looked back. For a good two minutes they had tried to stare each other out. Then they had gone to bed and let their bodies do the talking. It wasn't conventional police behaviour but she let herself be swept up in it. They talked about running away to Spain together. It had been a crazy time in her life. He was as mad as Mike himself in his own way, but he was married and wasn't sure about dumping the wife. So Angela enjoyed the sex while it lasted and kissed him goodbye. Look me up if you ever come back this way, he had said. She could not even remember his name.

Angela pulled herself to her feet and shuffled out into the aisle. She could not work the catch on her locker and finally somebody else reached over to open it. The unsolicited act made her realise she was drunk. She straightened her shoulders and began to take deep breaths, following the queue of slow-moving passengers off the plane, up the tunnel, through the corridors and finally down the steps into the arrivals hall where a sea of upturned faces waited.

She had phoned Gus from Heathrow, told him the time of the shuttle and asked him to collect her. There he was, a little apart from the main crowd, slightly embarrassed it seemed, but smiling genuinely as he tried to wave to her without anybody else noticing.

What was she doing here? Gus looked so like Mike standing there it frightened her. The brothers were so alike physically, yet complete opposites psychologically. Mike had been a doer. Gus was a fixer. Mike had been an unstable incendiary, Gus was a real slow-burning fuse.

She was glad Gus didn't see when a tear suddenly leaked spontaneously from the corner of her eye. She was able to brush it nonchalantly away with a fingertip. Memories of Mike often struck her like that, teasing her with visions of lost opportunities and the wasted potential of her life. The what-might-have-beens if his get-rich-quick scheme had worked first time out drove her crazy. If he hadn't been so impatient, if he hadn't killed himself rather than face prison, he would have been back with her now and the two of them could have ridden off into the sunset together and lived happily ever after. She would never have deserted Mike. She would have been the dutiful wife.

She hurried over to Gus, colliding with a few bodies in the crowd, threw her arms round him dramatically and kissed him hard on the lips.

'Welcome home,' he said.

'Nice to be here,' she replied, hanging on to his arm. 'What have you got for me?'

'For you I've got a big surprise.'

40

On the landing at the top of the stairs Mark Munro used the point of his index finger to push the door open. It moved sluggishly, held back by the carpet underneath its bottom edge.

'Tut, tut,' he said, stroking the splintered jamb. 'Looks like somebody forgot their key.'

Fyfe hesitated on the threshold and looked back over his shoulder at the door opposite. He had a feeling of being watched, of his every movement being observed by hidden eyes. He shook it off and followed Munro inside the flat to be followed himself by two other detective constables, Charlie Bain and Pete Crichton, and an elderly uniformed sergeant called Bill Campsie. The five of them stood together in the main room. The space was so cramped none of them could turn round without bumping into the others.

'Cosy,' Fyfe said.

'Empty,' Munro added. He had to stoop under the steep lie-in of the wall. 'I think we can safely say he isn't here without too extensive a search. There don't seem to be many hiding places. Charlie, Pete, do a round of the neighbours. See if anybody knows where Mr Adamson is and what he has been up to.'

Bain and Crichton made for the doorway, both trying to go through it at the same time and, in the best traditions of farce, having to readjust and draw back when they got stuck. Campsie waited until the misunderstanding was resolved, exchanged exasperated glances with his superiors, and strolled out casually, pulling the door shut behind him.

Fyfe sat on the mattress on the bed. Munro moved into the centre of the room where he had the air space to stand. Muffled voices came from outside, and the distant sound of a door bell.

'What do you think, then, Dave?'

'Curiouser and curiouser.'

'I think we're on the right track. I can smell something rotten. We're not far away here. Can you remember anything about Adamson? What kind of guy is he?'

'It's been nine years since we put him away,' Fyfe said. 'The case was a cracker; big money, blazing guns, sealed-off streets, Mad Mike blowing his head off, headlines six inches high. Adamson was the fall guy really. Hired muscle brought in at the last moment to carry some hardware and drive the getaway car. They hid the money in a half-built house that was burned down the same night they were arrested. It was set off by a booby trap that sprayed high octane petrol over all the walls. Everything inside was incinerated.'

'You believe that?'

'I didn't at first but we never did manage to break his story. Some bits of charred notes were found to back it up. Forensic said the intensity of the blaze was sufficient to vaporise paper. Adamson said Mike Barrie had set a booby trap on the cash and Forensic confirmed that was how it started. You know the kind, a candle burning down until it triggers an explosion. If they weren't going to have the money, the bank wasn't going to get it back. He said they had a suicide pact but he bottled out once he saw Mike's head explode.'

'But do you believe it, Dave?'

'Not at first. I, like many others, assumed he was a chancer. What finally convinced me is the fact that he has survived in prison all these years. If he had stashed the cash in a safe haven for his coming-out party I think big brother Gus Barrie might have had a quiet word with him before now.'

'Is he a murderer?'

'With a little encouragement I'm sure we all are. I was always suspicious about Mad Mike's death. I had this theory at the time that Adamson might have killed him to make sure he got out alive, but nobody else seemed to think much of it. And there wasn't any evidence, of course.'

'If we wanted a conviction without evidence we could have sent him south to be tried in the English courts.'

'There were just the two of them in that room,' Fyfe continued. 'Just the two, like you and me here now. If I was to take your gun, put it under your chin and pull the trigger then rapidly wipe all prints, stick the gun in your hand and fall on the floor a gibbering wreck, shocked by the sight of exploding human brains, I would get a lot of sympathy, I'll tell you.'

Munro rubbed his chin. 'Okay, let's come up to date. Where does this bloody dead priest fit in?'

Fyfe shrugged. 'Somewhere between the Devil and the slate grey sea.'

The door burst open and Crichton stood in front of them. His eyes were protruding, his cheeks were red and he was panting heavily.

'I think you should come and see this, sir,' Crichton almost shouted before promptly turning round and hurrying out.

Fyfe and Munro looked at each other quizzically and then followed, making sure they didn't collide in the doorway. The door opposite on the landing was open and they were waved inside and directed towards the sound of running water and the steam clouds pouring from the bathroom. Munro was first in, Fyfe close behind. The cubicle door was open. The body was squashed into a corner. An arm extended from it with the wrist at a ninety degree angle. Four fingertips of the other hand were pressed hard against the opaque plastic wall forming a curve of bullet holes. A crust of red and black blood was on the edge of the shower tray.

'Jesus Christ,' Munro said in a hoarse stage whisper.

'She's dead, sir,' Bain reported. 'Not very long ago. The water has kept her warm but she's stone dead. From the neck wound it looks like she's been garrotted too. I think I broke her wrist when I forced the sliding door open. I had to. She might have been alive.'

Munro nodded. 'Contact Forensic. We'll need more men here.'

'Done it. The outside door wasn't locked, sir. I could hear the shower running and I saw the steam through the letter box.'

Munro kept nodding. 'Any idea who she is?'

'Not yet, sir.'

'A neighbour of John Adamson. Not a healthy thing to be, obviously.'

Fyfe reached into the cubicle and turned off the shower, using the side of his hand to avoid smudging potential prints that would already have been ruined by the steam. The rushing sound was replaced by a steady metronome dripping. Pat, pat, pat, pat, pat.

Fyfe stared down on the wet mass of red hair and the white-skinned body. A spasm of nausea gurgled briefly in his gullet. He swallowed it. A sudden wave of weariness sucked the strength from him. He wondered if she would have been alive if Adamson had not been freed on parole — as he would not have been if Lord Greenmantle hadn't been in a good mood because sexy Sylvia had agreed to marry him because Fyfe was a married man and wouldn't commit himself. In a roundabout sort of way the death of this woman, maybe the priest too, was his fault.

'Bodies round every corner,' Fyfe said but nobody was listening. 'Milestones along the way.'

41

Angela was floating naked in the swimming pool, lying on her back looking up at the glass roof streaked by rain and tumbling leaves and other wind-blown debris. She moved her arms and legs no more than was necessary to remain on the surface of the deliciously warm water. She was totally relaxed. Her mind wandered freely, plotting her future in faraway places where she could be alone. The most important things the money would buy would be privacy and solitude. She would go where no one would find her. She would have a big villa in the sun, very like this one, surrounded by a high wall and inside the wall she would become a recluse. Everyone, but everyone, would be shut out. Even Gus. The poor sucker would take it hard. He was nice enough, and rich. But he was a man, a deadly boring man and there was no way round that. She was tired of living her life to please other people. It was time she pleased herself. If only she could have the chance.

She knew that Gus Barrie was watching her from the side of the pool, appreciative of every inch of flesh being displayed in front of him. She flaunted it shamelessly, enjoying herself, aware that the sight of her spread-eagled there was causing him to drool with animal lust. He sat with a glass of champagne in one hand and the other in his trouser pocket, massaging himself gently.

He was more obsessed with her than ever. She could see it in his eyes and sense it in the self-denying, hands-off manner he had been displaying since the airport. The welcoming kiss had made no impression on him. Snuggling up to him in the car had produced no response. She didn't believe him about the money, but didn't really care anyway. She would be able to get a decent return out of him. On arrival at the house he had suggested a swim and she had expected him to come to the bedroom to claim his due as she changed. The house was empty, he kept insisting. They were the only two people in it.

She liked the house. The follow-you-around lights and music were wonderful. The television in her bedroom was voice-activated but once she had switched it on it wouldn't go off. She left her swimming costume in her suitcase, knowing the effect bare flesh would have on him, and went down in a towelling robe. He was sitting at a table laid with a light lunch by the side of the pool. He had a bottle of champagne ready too. Expensive stuff that went straight to her head. She had prepared herself for an early session of unsubtle pawing and clawing, but he didn't seem to want to touch her. That suited her fine. She liked being put on a pedestal. She liked it when men only looked, wide-eyed and clueless, looked but did not touch.

Gus was perhaps reverting to his second adolescence. He was probably building up to another of his agonisingly embarrassing proposals of marriage. She would have to be careful in the way she turned it down this time. Jealousy and rejection were powerful emotions that could drive a man to desperate acts. She had come all this way to be with him. His hopes would be high. Still, it was good to make Gus sweat. It would leach the poisons out of his system. It would make him a better person. He could stand it. She was good for him.

Angela kicked her legs to stay afloat and moved slowly through the water. Gus probably had a subconscious desire to emulate his younger brother. Young Mike had been the baby of the family, the spoiled child, his mummy's favourite. Gus had always considered himself second best; not so handsome, not so dynamic, not so devil-may-care.

He had been the boring, predictable one. Mike had been the extrovert the women loved. Big brother Gus, very much second choice.

The phone on the poolside table began to pulse. Barrie did not take his eyes off Angela in the water as he answered it. Angela rolled on her front and kicked with her legs, opening them wide and bringing them together smartly to drift away from him. When she rolled over again the call was finished.

'Visitors?' she asked.

'Visitors bearing gifts.'

'For me?'

She twisted round and grabbed hold of the side of the pool, lifting herself out in one fluid motion. Barrie was instantly on his feet and had a towel ready for her.

'Now I can keep my promise,' he said. 'Get dressed and come back down to see what I have got.' He blew a kiss as she hurried away. 'See what I have got. Especially for you.'

42

The murder of the redhead was hot news. It pointed the finger at a prime suspect in John Adamson. He had a history of involvement in violent crime and had been released from prison only the previous day. Fyfe could see the minds snapping shut all around him. The case was solved. All that remained was to find their man. After a brief burst of self-congratulation the minds had to be prised open again. It dawned on them that Adamson had still been behind bars when Ross Sorley had been taken out, and Georgie Boy Craig and his boyfriend. The perfect alibi. A guest of Her Majesty. So if they got Adamson for the priest and the redhead, they were no nearer having a name in the frame for the other three murders. Yet the way the redhead had been killed carried the drugs war trademark. She presumably had the dead priest to thank for her accommodation, and the priest had collected Adamson from Saughton Prison personally. There had to be a connection somewhere.

Mark Munro massaged his temples forcefully and willed inspiration to come. Detectives hunting in pairs fanned out and began door-to-door inquiries. The mobile incident room was brought in and parked half on the pavement and half off it outside the tenement. Munro liked to lead from the front so he stayed out while Fyfe went back to oversee the setting up of an inquiry data base.

The Gothic architecture of Fettes College on the low hill above the police headquarters was a familiar landmark Fyfe homed in on from the other side of the city. It was after midday and the tip of the central spire was hidden by a canopy of murky low cloud. Cars drove with their headlights turned on to penetrate the daytime gloom. He still hadn't eaten anything since waking up with Sylvia on his back, but hunger had slipped way down his list of priorities. He was thinking about his conversation with Lord Greenmantle as they sat by the fire staring out the window. 'All sorts of things are happening out there,' the judge had said. 'Deliberate, accidental, circumstantial.' Into which category did the murder of the priest and the execution of the redhead fall? Which one of them had said, 'The wonder is we ever make sense of all the chaos'?

Fyfe felt hollow, not from any lack of food but from a terrible sense of foreboding. Things were happening out there and his personal life seemed to be all muddled in with his professional life. The priest in the park and the redhead in the shower were the lucky ones. They didn't have to worry about anything any more.

He hadn't told anyone about Greenmantle's reasons for sanctioning Adamson's parole. It would take some explaining before outsiders would be able to understand that Fyfe himself was the catalyst that had allowed Adamson back on the streets. Adamson had no obvious link with drugs but he had been the partner of Mad Mike Barrie whose brother Gus, despite a snow white criminal record, was the biggest drug baron in the country. It would no doubt emerge that the redhead was a reformed junkie and small-time dealer. She had been Adamson's neighbour, part of the rehabilitation project the accountant Fleming had exposed as so rotten. The priest Byrne had been benefactor to both of them. A faint pattern was slowly establishing itself on the bewildering chaos, fleeting glimpses of substance in the fog. Fyfe was an essential part of it.

The sight of the redhead's fragile body crammed into the shower cubicle had affected him badly. At every moment he had expected her to begin coughing as life returned. That was what had happened with Sally when she was attacked. He had watched her from the distance through the shattered window, the thin strip of metal he was balanced on boring painfully into the soles of his feet. She had lain so still, her skin smeared with somebody else's blood, and he had believed she was dead. But then after several endless seconds life had come back. Air forced itself into her lungs and her whole body had trembled with the painful shock of it. He had thought the same thing would happen with the redhead. He expected her to raise her head and gasp for breath. He was still waiting for it to happen when the scene of crime was marked off, the photographs were taken, and the body was finally zipped up in a purple vinyl bag and carried down the stairs.

Fyfe entered the headquarters building by a side door. Since the morning, the main incident room on the ground floor had been kick-started out of its lethargy and transformed into a bustling factory floor of activity. Officers in starched white shirts strode about purposefully with pieces of paper in their hands. There were many more crimes than random murders being committed out there. The weekend was always the busiest time.

148

Ronnie McGregor, the uniformed assistant chief constable in charge of administration, met Fyfe at the entrance and guided him to a side office created from partition walls that stopped three foot short of the ceiling. A rectangle of card with the title Co-ordinator written on it had been inserted in the slot on the door. Sir Duncan Morrison, the Chief Constable, had insisted on Fyfe being given the title so he could feel important with Munro still in overall charge. Fyfe was flattered and suspicious at being treated so sensitively. Maybe he knew too much and they wanted to keep him on their side.

Co-ordinator. Fyfe mouthed the word, breaking it into five syllables and enjoying the sound of it. Not as snappy as troubleshooter, but getting there.

'Do you think he was knocking her off, then?' asked McGregor, who liked to think he was one of the boys.

'Who?'

'The priest?'

'Priests don't do that sort of thing.'

'They don't get their brains bashed out in Holyrood Park either. Me? I reckon it's a jealous lover on the loose.'

'I'll add the theory to the data base, sir.'

'Christ's sake, imagine discovering your woman's being poked by a priest. Is nothing sacred? Don't touch the computer for twenty minutes. The engineers are working on the system or something. You'll find a bunch of files in there. Shout if you need any more.'

Fyfe flopped down in his new office. It was tiny, barely five foot square. The walls were blank. The desk supported a monitor, keyboard, telephone, and a pile of folders in a single wire basket. He tried the telephone but it was dead. There was not enough space to do a full turn in the swivel seat. The urgent murmur of the incident room beyond spilled over the top of the walls.

Fyfe looked at his face on the dark screen and wondered when Father Byrne and the redhead had died. Had he been sitting beside the fire at Sylvia's sipping strong whisky when the priest plummeted over the crags? Had he been locked in sexual union with Sylvia when the razor wire was slicing through the redhead's throat? He noticed that the jackplug for the phone was not inserted in the socket, so he reached down and fixed it. A loud dialling tone burred in his ear. He punched the correct digits to have calls diverted from his extension in the Fraud Squad office.

There was a knock at the door and the walls wobbled. Sir Duncan put his head round. 'David, we have a new ball game,' he said.

'So it would seem, sir.'

'I've already told the Archbishop.'

Fyfe nodded. Sir Duncan did not try to enter. He stood in the doorway with his arms folded like a bouncer blocking the way.

'I want you to take the press conference scheduled for three with Detective Superintendent Munro,' Sir Duncan said. 'We will release the names then. I don't want you to tell them anything concrete, just haver convincingly. You're good at that.'

Fyfe didn't know whether to take the remark as a compliment or not so he ignored it. Sir Duncan was distracted, as though the rash of murders were interfering with matters of greater importance on his mind. Fyfe knew the feeling.

'We have our own case conference at two,' Fyfe said. 'Detective Superintendent Munro will be back to take it. Do you want me to feed the media hyenas anything about the possible links between the murders?'

'Explain to me what ties this lot in a package?' Sir Duncan said.

'Five people dead in two days, four killed by the same method. The dumbest reporter is going to ask the obvious question. And the other a priest who runs off the edge of Salisbury Crags to be battered to death at the bottom. He happens to have a close connection with one of the murder victims. That's why I'm the co-ordinator, I assume.'

Sir Duncan looked at the card on the door and laughed a little.

'It's a juicy story whatever we say,' Fyfe continued. 'Better to steer them in the right direction. Don't you agree?'

'Of course, of course. Prepare a draft statement and let me see it.'

'I wasn't thinking about a written statement.' What am I, he thought? Your fucking office boy? 'I would just do it by answering the obvious questions in a certain way.'

'What are the obvious questions?' Sir Duncan asked disingenuously.

'What the hell is going on and why are all these people dead?'

The phone rang. Sir Duncan frowned and retreated. 'Speak to me before the press conference,' he said.

It was Catriona on the phone. Her intervention wrenched Fyfe's attention from the inquiry. She wanted to know when he was going to collect his dogs because she had to go out for the evening. The tone of her voice showed that she was annoyed at being taken for granted and having them dumped on her. Jill and Number Five were, she said, lying sleeping on the sofa and what was he going to do about it? He tried to explain he was really busy but soon realised she wasn't going to stand for it. She hadn't heard of any murders in the city. That was a million miles removed from the world she lived in. Fyfe promised to pick up the dogs before five o'clock.

He put the phone down and it rang again immediately. Hearing Brother Patrick speak refocused Fyfe's attention on the death of Father Byrne. He had made a mental note to contact the Tayside retreat. It was logical that Father Quinn would have to be interviewed again as soon as possible.

'Ah Mr Fyfe. Sad news.' The voice seemed to come from a great distance, as if somebody was shouting across a vast plain.

'What's the problem, Brother?' Fyfe asked, amused at the unintentional hand-slapping rhythm of the question.

'Father Quinn is no longer with us.'

'What do you mean? Has he left?' By the time he had blurted out the two sentences Fyfe had figured it out for himself. 'You mean he's dead.'

'Sadly, yes. He slipped out to the cliffs early this morning while we were at prayers. I returned just in time to see him throw himself off. All our efforts have been in vain. May he rest in peace.'

Fyfe created a mind picture of the scene. Brother Patrick standing at the window in his Reeboks, arms folded into his sleeves, looking out over the savagely jagged coastline with the slate-grey sea sucking and clutching at the base of the rocks. Quinn on the edge of the cliffs, spreading his arms and jumping. His puny body momentarily magnified as it passed through the flaws in the glass of the window panes and then swiftly diminished by the distance of the fall into the unforgiving water far below and the lethal rocks. Another broken body to add to the count.

Quinn must have been sneaking out to his death around the time Fyfe was making his excuses and leaving Sylvia. It did not rule him out as a suspect for Byrne's murder, or the redhead's for that matter. How tidy it would be if they could pin the blame on a renegade priest. Why else would Quinn commit suicide? Surely a visit from a detective would not be enough to push him over the edge. Archbishop Delaney would approve. The scandal would be neatly wrapped up and placed in the bin.

'The lifeboat has recovered his body,' Brother Patrick was saying. 'He had multiple injuries from being washed against the rocks. It would be a mercy if he drowned first. There was nothing we could do.'

'Did he leave any note or anything?'

'Nothing.'

'He didn't say anything after I left yesterday?'

'No. Do not blame yourself, DCI Fyfe. He could no longer abide his sinful existence. I knew you would want to know. God will have mercy on his soul.'

Brother Patrick was gone before Fyfe had the chance to tell him what had happened to Byrne. He looked up the number in his diary and phoned back. The monk said he was shocked but it did not shake his calm demeanour. Fyfe threw in the redhead with her throat cut gratuitously to try and provoke a reaction. 'God will have mercy on their souls,' Brother Patrick repeated sonorously. There was no possibility that Quinn had left the retreat during the previous evening. The only way out was by motor vehicle and there were none there, except for the mini tractors. If there had been the commotion of a departure it could not have gone unnoticed.

'Seems he didn't have blood on his conscience then,' Fyfe said.

'No,' Brother Patrick replied. 'There must be another sinner loose in this world.'

When the conversation was over Fyfe adjusted his shoulders to bear the weight of the new monkey on his back. He imagined Brother Patrick putting down the phone, sliding his hands into his sleeves and padding off in air-cushioned silence.

43

'Come down now, Angela darling.' Barrie's voice spoke over the bedroom intercom, competing with the jabbering television. 'We're waiting for you in the games room.'

Angela had dried her hair in the bedroom and painted on a face: dark eyes, highlighted cheekbones, wet scarlet lips. She took her time because she wanted to look her best. This moment had been a long time coming. Once it was over maybe Mike would finally be laid to rest and she could get away and get on with her life.

She found the dress she was looking for in one of her suitcases. It was made from clinging crushed velvet, black and short with a low-cut neck, and gave the desired spray-paint effect. She didn't bother with underwear. She admired herself in the full-length mirror, smoothing the dress over her thighs and puffing out her chest so that her nipples were clearly defined. 'Knock them dead, girl,' she told herself. 'Knock them dead.'

Her stiletto heels clicked sharply on the parquet floors of the curving corridor and down the ringing cast iron of the spiral staircase. The glass walls of the games room were blanked out by the reflection of the water in the swimming pool. Somebody, a distorted shape, was moving behind it. Two people? Two shapes? No. Three shapes? A fourth? Or maybe it was all a trick of the light.

It was a shame the pleasurable fantasy about the pot of gold at the end of the memory rainbow was about to end. For nine years she had lived with the dream that she only had to reach back to collect what was rightfully hers. She had never believed it, the same way she had never believed Mike was actually dead. Nine years was an eternity to keep a simple hope alive but she had managed it because there had been no one to deny it entirely. It had been her escape route all this time. The pension fund nobody back in Spain knew about. The non-existent fund she had been counting on all these years. A pleasing fantasy it had been. She would almost have preferred to continue with it rather than have it killed stone dead.

Too late for such faint-heartedness now. Gus had promised her a surprise. She hesitated at the threshold, smoothed out her dress for a final time. The truth was about to crawl out from under its stone. 'Gentlemen,' she said. 'I believe you have something to tell me.'

Gus Barrie went over to her and took her by the hand. He led her forward to the snooker table where three black plastic sacks were stacked together among the scattered balls. On the opposite side Billy Jones was licking the cube of blue chalk. His brother Sandy was standing further apart, lifting weights on the multi-gym. Angela could just see his hands and waist through the gap between the table and the fringed hanging light canopy. The table surface was in dark shadow. She reached out and touched the neck of one of the sacks.

Barrie introduced the Jones brothers by name. They nodded and stared openly at her. Sandy sneezed. John Adamson was introduced and smiled pathetically. Angela did not recognise him. He had aged too much. He looked nothing like the ferret-faced person she vaguely remembered. 'Mr Adamson has brought this present for you, Angela,' Barrie said. 'Haven't you, John?'

Adamson was standing sideways on to the table, his shoulder against the canopy, making it sway slightly. He held out his hand uncertainly but she did not take it. His fingers dropped down to drum silently on the end of a cue lying on the green baize surface. Lizard-like, his eyes darted from side to side.

Angela stared at the bulging sacks. Excitement gagged in her throat. Could it be that Gus had been telling the truth all along? The money did exist? Her money? She was suddenly homesick for the sunshine and security of Spain.

'Jad, isn't it?' she said. 'I remember you well, Jad. You and Mike were friends.'

'Friends and colleagues,' he replied.

'You killed him.'

Adamson's jaw fell and his hands shot up like someone offering to surrender. 'No. No. I was there when he shot himself. I didn't shoot him.'

'That's what I meant.'

Angela gained a little satisfaction from Adamson's discomfiture, a minuscule piece of revenge for Mike's death. She felt supremely confident and totally in control with the eyes of all four men roaming over her tightly wrapped body. She was in her element but it was obvious Adamson was not present in the room from his own free will. There was a bruise on the side of his head and his top lip was slightly swollen. Gus had something planned and she could guess exactly what it was. It was so unnecessary, so wasteful. Just like Mike's death in the first place. Somehow it was also appropriate.

'I didn't kill him,' Adamson insisted.

'I believe you,' she said quietly, almost apologetically. She smoothed her dress over her hips and wished she had put on underwear. She was not properly dressed for the occasion.

'Why don't you show Angela what's in here, Jad?' Barrie said. 'Billy, lights, please.'

The black sacks and the green baize and the scatter of coloured balls became bathed in white light. Barrie punched the side of a sack as if it was somebody's cheek.

'Of course, of course,' Adamson said. He quickly tore open the neck of the sack nearest to him and bundles of banknotes poured out on to the table. The snooker balls clicked together as they were disturbed.

'It's all there, Angela,' Barrie said eagerly. 'All the money Mike stole, every last fiver of it. Jad showed us where it was hidden. Didn't you, Jad?'

'Yes. I did.'

'It wasn't destroyed at all. It was a trick to fool the police and the bank. It worked. Everybody believed for these last nine years that it went up in smoke. But here it is and it's yours, just like I promised. Didn't I tell you I would look after you, Angela? Didn't I tell you?'

Angela stared at the brown and purple avalanche of banknotes. Then at Adamson. Then at Barrie. It couldn't be true. There had to be some catch to this. And yet the evidence was in front of her eyes, crisp and bright. After nine years shouldn't the colours have faded a bit? Her mind seized on the doubt.

'Tell her, Jad,' Barrie ordered.

'This is your money, Mrs Barrie,' Adamson said, nodding frantically. 'I hid it away. I didn't tell anyone. I kept it a secret until I was out of prison and now I've collected it and brought it back for you.'

'Isn't that nice of him, Angela?' Barrie said. 'He's brought it back for you. It didn't even occur to him to keep it for himself.'

Adamson's nodding turned into a confirmatory shaking of the head. The hanging canopy over the snooker table swung as he kept bumping it with his shoulder. There was a pause, a moment of utter stillness. A chill entered the atmosphere, freezing the air the way water is transformed from a liquid to a solid and becomes ice. Adamson shivered. The canopy swung.

'Actually it did occur to the conniving bastard,' Barrie said. 'In fact, if we hadn't found him I'm sure he would have tried to protect his little secret. If we hadn't found him he would never have thought of returning the money to its rightful owner.'

Adamson kept shaking his head. Sandy Jones had left the weights and was moving round the table. The leather handles on the razor wire were wound round his fists. Adamson hadn't seen him. Barrie pulled on her elbow and Angela took a step backwards.

'He wasn't going to bring the money back for you, Angela,' Barrie said, his voice rising. 'He was going to keep Mike's money for himself. He had been planning it for nine years. But it didn't work. Oh no. I stopped him. I got your money back for you, Angela. I kept my promise to you.'

Adamson was beginning to crouch over like an athlete at the start of a race. The bombs were screaming about his head, about to explode. Barrie's nostrils were twitching furiously. There were little patches of foam at the corners of his mouth. Angela took another step backwards.

'Now you can have the head of John Adamson,' Barrie shouted. 'Do it.'

44

The joke about priests falling from grace wasn't funny after a while. When Mark Munro got back and learned that the sad-faced Father Quinn had gone to meet his maker the first thing he did was crack the joke. No one laughed. He was disappointed when Fyfe told him the monks would swear Quinn never left home.

Fyfe had battered most of the information from criminal records into the new computer file. Most of it was available by electronic transfer from the force's mainframe so it did not take long. Most of it was probably unhelpful but could not be ignored at such an early stage. Fyfe's hardest job was to think of a codename for the inquiry file. After ten minutes of pen chewing and his thoughts wandering abstractly over Sylvia climbing on top of him in the fireside chair and Jill and Number Five sleeping peacefully on the sofa he came up with Sleeping Dogs. He typed it into the identification panel and hoped nobody would ask why.

Pete Crichton squeezed into the office and offered the first scrap of real information supplied by a batty old dear on the ground floor who kept lists of the numbers of every car parked in the street she didn't recognise.

'She said it would come in useful some day,' Crichton said, taking pleasure in describing her as an old white-haired witch with twinkling eyes and a constant dribble of saliva on to her chin. 'Very public-spirited she is.'

'A neighbourhood watch freak and a half,' Fyfe said. 'I'll bet most of them are illicit leg-over situations.'

The list had only four numbers on it. Fyfe typed them into the terminal and asked for the owners' names and addresses but there was some kind of hitch with the linkup to Swansea. The machine kept asking him to try again. He still hadn't made contact by two o'clock when Munro called everyone together in an empty seminar room on the first floor. There were about forty people and half that number of seats. Munro stood up front, Sir Duncan and Ronnie McGregor sat on opposite edges of the table like book-ends. Fyfe stood at the back, leaning against the wall.

A roll call of the dead had been compiled on the display board. Photographs, full frontal and profile, had been culled from criminal records and blown up to just short of life size. Ross Sorley appeared at one end of the row. Then there was Georgie Craig, looking mean and butch, and a distinctly effeminate Michael Ellis. All three had convictions for possession of and dealing in Class A controlled drugs. The redhead had been identified as Lillian Sherwin, born in Glasgow, two convictions for possession of hard drugs and one for dealing cannabis. Her unflattering likeness, sunken eyes and hair scraped back, had been dug out of the files too and was pinned beside a smiling head and shoulders of Father Byrne provided by the Church. John Adamson was given pride of place on a level of his own above the rogues' gallery. Only Father Quinn remained anonymous. As an afterthought, Munro drew a matchstick man on a sheet of white paper and added him to the side.

'We have a prime suspect,' Munro said.

He reached up to touch Adamson's face on the board and left a black mark on one cheek. He rehearsed the histories of each victim, the Church funds fiddle, and the connections which linked all five. Circumstantial evidence comprehensively damned Adamson for the murders of Byrne and the redhead but cleared him on the first three charges. Father Quinn was a wild card.

'Drugs are involved in this somewhere,' Munro said. 'The razor wire neck-ties are an unsubtle tribal war-cry. The word from the streets through our usual contacts is confused as yet but no doubt it will get clearer. Until then I intend to concentrate on finding Adamson. We find him and hopefully we find the key to the truth. There is a weird logic in all this, if no sense. Let's treat it like a cryptic crossword clue. It will be so simple once the code is broken and the correct answer revealed. We'll toss Adamson's name into the pool and see what ripples it makes.'

There was no applause after the pep-talk, just a few raised eyebrows at the flowery language. Munro had always been a bit of a showman in his own laid-back fashion. The meeting had lasted half an hour. It broke up with everybody speculating freely about randy priests, sexy redheads, and crazed stranglers. Senior officers at DCI level and above remained, gathering in front of the photographs on the wall like visitors at an art gallery.

'Do you think the dead priest was crooked?' Munro asked Fyfe.

'Which one?'

'Why does Adamson do him and the woman, that's what I'd like to know.' Munro was talking to himself.

'A jealous love rival?' Fyfe suggested. 'If the bastard was fiddling the money, it seems reasonable he could just as easily have been fiddling the women. But then I'm getting my priests mixed up. Quinn was the guilty one. Byrne turned him in and has the Archbishop's blessing.'

'Some blessing, a shattered skull.'

'Mysterious ways, Mark. Mysterious ways.'

'Anyway, any hard information come in yet, Coordinator?'

'Just the disk in the computer,' Fyfe replied. 'That's the hardest thing in this investigation so far.'

The room emptied. Fyfe got back to his cubby-hole just as the direct line rang. He grabbed it, sat down, and set the computer searching for the list of car numbers in one movement. Sylvia was on the other end. The smile that jumped on to his face was entirely spontaneous. Dead bodies fled his consciousness to be replaced by warm-blooded living ones.

'It won't work, Dave,' Sylvia said.

'What won't?'

'You and me. The arrangement we talked about. It won't work. I think we should finish it here and now.'

Fyfe took a set of house keys from his pocket and tumbled them over and over between his fingers. His smile slowly dissolved. The terminal asked him to try again. He thumped the keyboard.

'It was your idea, Sylvia,' he said.

'Yes, I know and it was a mistake. It won't work. It can't work. I'm sorry but I should never have bothered you.'

'Bothered me. Is that what you call it?'

'Like I said, we should have let sleeping dogs lie.'

'Should we?' He frowned at the title of the inquiry file flashing on the screen in front of him.

'Don't make this difficult for me, Dave. I should never have... We should never have... It was a daft idea. I'm sorry.'

'I thought you'd talked it over with Lord Graeme?'

'I had.'

'And again? This change of mind, have you talked that over with him?'

'No. I've decided I don't want to have an affair with you. Not again. I just want to be friends. We have empathy, you and I. Why do we need sex?'

Fyfe suppressed a hysterical impulse to bawl down the phone to show Sylvia how funny he found everything. But laughter sneaked out, spilling like crumbs of food from an over-full mouth. He sat up straight, composing himself, swallowing his pride and his laughter.

'I rather fancied the idea of another steamy affair with you,' he said. 'Especially after last night. I enjoyed that. Didn't you?'

'It was crazy.'

'I enjoyed it anyway.'

'You're making this hard for me, Dave. Please don't turn up at the party tonight.'

'Okay. I know when I'm not wanted.'

'Thanks. I've got to go, Dave.' She was suddenly impatient. 'I'll speak to you soon. I do want to be friends. I don't want to lose you.'

'You've lost me,' Fyfe said, instantly regretting the words, desperate to retract them. 'I mean, I don't understand. See you sometime.'

Fyfe threw down the phone and rocked back in his chair. The world was going mad around him. He thought of Donald Byrne falling down a cliff face, followed by Richard Quinn, and saw himself falling after them. A list of four names and addresses scrolled down the screen. Three meant nothing to him, the fourth was the owner of a Ford Transit van. Windfall Construction. Who owned Windfall Construction? Gus Barrie. Inappropriate laughter threatened to overwhelm Fyfe once more. It was all so inevitable. He covered his face with his hands. He was angry, depressed, disappointed and confused.

The walls of the tiny cubicle quivered as Mark Munro pushed the door open and stood blocking the doorway. Fyfe looked out from between his fingers.

'Ready for the fray?' Munro asked. 'The media are waiting. Let's do it to them before they do it to us.'

45

Adamson could see what was intended from the moment Barrie started spouting the fantasy about the money being reincarnated. He was as mad as his brother had been, only Mike was the self-destructive type. Gus Barrie took out his frustrations on other people.

Adamson put on a genuine show of nervousness, playing along with Barrie's sick game, but all the time he was assessing the options open to him. They thought he was a lamb to the slaughter, a helpless sacrificial victim who would not put up a fight when he was dispatched in front of a honey blonde with a blood red mouth and a slinky black dress. Well, he was no victim. He was a killer like them. Only last night he had killed a man. He could kill plenty more.

It was dark outside. He had guessed it was about six in the evening when the skinhead brothers marched him up the driveway through an avenue of trees. He had been locked in a bathroom after Barrie's lecture on how to behave. All he could hear were the sounds of the pigeons scratching and strutting above him and one of the brothers sniffing and sneezing on the other side of the door.

They had held on to his upper arms and wrists in a very professional manner. Their feet had crunched loudly on the rough gravel, legs moving in perfect synchronisation. The big house was impressive, the indoor swimming pool even more so. A heavy glass wall was pushed to one side and he stepped over the ridge. Barrie had been playing one of the pinball machines. The three sacks of money were propped up together on the snooker table. The brothers had moved into the background. 'Remember what I told you?' Barrie had asked in a confidential whisper. And then they waited until the glass wall was sliding open once more and Mad Mike's widow was high-stepping into the room. For a brief instant as she soaked up everybody's attention he had considered making a dash for freedom but fear had weakened his muscles. They would not react to commands from his brain. He had been rooted firmly to the spot. He still was.

The bombs started to go off around Adamson as Barrie's intention became more and more clear. The high-pitched screech of their imagined falling ripped through his brain, making him grimace. Involuntarily, he folded into a semi-crouching position. Sandy Jones was behind him, breathing harshly. When Barrie ordered him to act Sandy sneezed. Adamson felt the wetness on the back of his neck and it was the spur that sent him somersaulting forward and spinning on his back, just missing the woman's legs. He swung the cue diagonally so that the lead-weighted end caught his attacker on the side of the head. The hollow thump of wood against bone froze Sandy Jones in mid-movement. The side of his face darkened instantaneously as if a cloud had obscured the sun. Blood splashed from the wound. It spattered down on to balled fists that held a vicious shining length of razor wire stretched tightly between them.

The sight of it gave Adamson adrenalin-fed speed and strength. He swung the cue in a circle round his head and struck Sandy's jaw with all the power he could summon up. It made a different sound, a crackling noise like something hard and brittle being crushed. Shock waves vibrated up Adamson's arm. The cue snapped and a lethally jagged edge impaled Sandy's throat, releasing a spout of blood. He fell sideways against the table but before he had rolled off on to the floor his brother Billy was jumping past him. Adamson kicked out but Billy was on him. The top of his skull hit Adamson under the chin and knocked him back. The force of the contact winded and dazed him. He lost his grip on the broken snooker cue and it bounced out of reach. He twisted desperately to escape from Billy's embrace, steeling himself for the expected punches or the sharp blade of a knife sliding between his ribs.

But nothing happened. Adamson's whole body prickled with dread anticipation. He could not understand why Billy just lay there, a dead-weight pinning him down. His soft leather jacket was curiously warm and damp at the back. Over his shoulder he could see Angela watching him and Barrie scampering round the edge of the table. The fringed canopy rocked. Barrie's face came into view and with it the gun he was holding.

With all the mind bombs exploding around him, Adamson had not heard the crack of the gunshot. But it explained the red stains on the palms of his hands and Billy's inertia on top of him. His instinctive defence of his brother had blocked the gunshot aimed at Adamson.

The realisation produced another surge of energy. Adamson squirmed out from under Billy and ducked behind a pinball machine. The crack of another shot sent a bullet ricocheting off the metal corner and humming round the room. The entire glass wall fronting on to the swimming pool shattered but stayed whole, like a car windscreen hit by a flying stone. Adamson ducked behind the next machine as the next bullet crashed into it, setting the mechanics in motion. A tinny vaudeville tune began to play and the bumpers rang and flashed as a ball was injected among them.

Adamson was aware he was a sitting target. He had no choice but to go on the offensive. There was not enough cover and not enough space in the room for him to hide.

He ran out from behind the echoing pinball machine and another bullet singed the air in front of his face. He kept running straight at Barrie, charging straight at the barrel of the ridiculously small handgun. Another shot. A crack as loud as a booming gong and a sharp pain low down in his chest.

But it did not slow him. It did not prevent him hitting Barrie hard in the midriff with his shoulder, slamming him backwards. They went straight through the opaque wall of bullet-shattered glass. It exploded at the first touch, disintegrating in a silvery cascade of blunt-edged shards that fell over them and bounced around them like hailstones. The momentum of their backward rush was not checked at all by the collision and they plunged into the swimming pool.

Adamson snatched a deep breath before going under but Barrie swallowed water and his struggling was immediately panic-stricken. Adamson had his hands on Barrie's throat and he kept them there. He climbed above him as they bobbed to the surface, using his head as a handhold, managing to gulp air to fill his lungs before they went down again. Barrie thrashed and writhed. His eyes bulged and bubbles streamed from his open mouth. Adamson simply clung to him, holding him under, knowing that he had the advantage. He could feel Barrie's strength draining away.

Once more they floated up and once more Adamson ensured that he was the only one to break the surface and reach the air. Barrie's attempts to break free redoubled, frantic and jerky, and for a moment Adamson thought he was not going to be able to restrain him. Then, abruptly, he weakened and the hands clawing at Adamson's face lost all urgency. Adamson held on, staying under the water until his lungs were entirely empty. Then he released the limp body and kicked away towards the light.

Barrie sank, drifting in the crucifix position, his knees scraping the bottom. Adamson rose, bursting up to relish the sensuous taste of the cold

163

air, but even as he did so the pain in his chest seemed to be acting as an anchor that was trying to drag him down. The water around him was pink from the loss of his own blood. He struck out to swim for the side and a teeth-gritting spasm of pain lanced through him. Three more muscle-wasting spasms shook him before he reached the side of the pool. His left arm was useless and, exhausted by the struggle, he could not pull himself out with only his right. He was close to tears, frustrated that he should get the better of three of the bastards and not be able to cash in. He hung on the side, panting, refusing to despair, preparing himself for one last supreme effort that would take him to safety.

It was several seconds before he noticed the high heels, and the legs, and the foreshortened, curve-enhanced body of Mike's widow standing over him.

He had forgotten about her.

Thank God.

She would help him.

46

The press conference was in the lecture hall on the third floor. Fyfe and Munro sat at the front with the blackboard behind them and the steeply pitched rows of seats in front. The crowd of faces stared down like reflections in a shattered mirror. A clutch of cameras occupied space in the forefront with photographers kneeling in front of them. Microphones and tape recorders cluttered the edge of the table that separated the two policemen from the mob. Two uniformed officers stood on either side of the door like bouncers handing out lists of names of the murder victims. Both Munro and Fyfe had been on media-handling courses. Adamson was to be a surprise. It would give the reporters a new line and keep them happy. They would be eating out of the police hand.

Munro coughed delicately to attract attention and the sound boomed out through the loudspeakers. The ranks of reporters fell silent. The cameramen ducked behind their machines. The sound engineers checked their levels.

The photographers fired their flashes like a volley of shots. Munro played the showman, introducing himself and Fyfe.

'Right, ladies and gentlemen,' he said. 'You will all be aware that in the last forty-eight hours there have been five murders in the city. You have a list of the names and what biographical details we possess. Pictures should be available by the time we finish here. I must stress that as things stand we have no evidence that there is any link at all between the five killings. However, it would not be an unreasonable assumption to make and I assume you have probably already assumed it.'

Munro waited for a reaction and there was a dutiful murmur of laughter. He kicked Fyfe's ankle under the table to prepare him to take over. The idea was to give them John Adamson's name without revealing he was a neighbour of the redhead. Cause of death was to be neck trauma or strangulation with no mention of near decapitation. Byrne's death was to be attributed to the fall from the crags and other injuries consistent with human intervention.

'As always we are keeping an open mind. I'll now hand over to Detective Chief Inspector David Fyfe who is acting as co-ordinator for the separate inquiries.'

The entire room's attention switched along the table. The cameras moved round on their tripods. Another volley of flashes was fired.

'At this early stage we have yet to establish many details,' Fyfe said, reading off the prepared statement that had been approved by Sir Duncan. 'However, in connection with our inquiries we would like to question John Adamson, a thirty-two-year-old white male who was released from Saughton Prison yesterday morning. Pictures of Adamson will be provided before you leave.'

They were all writing furiously, heads down. Fyfe looked up and smiled. Beyond them, a narrow window at the back showed a slice of dark grey sky. Things are happening out there, he thought. The raw material of future press conferences.

'Adamson was released on parole after serving nine years of a twelve-year sentence for armed robbery. His present whereabouts are unknown.'

Fyfe folded the piece of paper in half as he finished and sat back.

'Any questions?' Munro asked.

They all hesitated and then all began shouting simultaneously. Eventually they resorted to putting their hands up. Munro chose a young woman in the second row.

'Is this person Adamson suspected of the murders?'

'We believe Mr Adamson would be helpful in advancing our inquiries,' Munro said, moving on to a middle-aged man with a ravaged face and a drinker's nose directly behind her.

'Is this the guy that was involved in the gun siege all those years ago?'

'I understand that his arrest followed the discharge of a shotgun.'

'And you were one of the arresting officers, weren't you, Dave?'

Fyfe didn't recognise the reporter. 'Yes, I was,' he agreed.

He enjoyed the fact that he was the only person present who knew the real reason why Adamson had been let out on parole. Fyfe had kept the potential link to Gus Barrie to himself as well. Maybe it would turn out to be as tenuous as his own involvement in Adamson being set free.

'What's it all about?' the unknown reporter asked.

'Your guess is as good as mine.'

A television reporter butted in from the front row. 'This dead priest. Has a priest ever been murdered in the city before?'

Fyfe and Munro looked at each other. 'Ask the Church,' Munro said.

'Drugs. Is there a drug involvement?' somebody shouted from the rear.

'It is a possibility,' Fyfe said. He was thinking about the Transit van and Gus Barrie and the long-dead brother Mike and beautiful Angela and the soft touch of her foot rubbing against his leg.

'Is the neck trauma caused by garrottes of razor wire?'

'We cannot disclose the exact nature of the fatal injuries at the moment,' Munro said. 'Forensic tests have not been completed.'

'Was the priest a drug dealer?'

'Not as far as we know.'

'Is it being viewed as a drug war between rival gangs?'

'Not at this stage.'

'Wasn't this bloke Adamson the legman for Mad Mike Barrie?'

'He was arrested nine years ago after Barrie had shot himself. He was convicted of armed robbery.'

'A million quid, wasn't it?'

'Substantially more.'

'And it was never recovered.'

'It was incinerated in a fire. We found the ashes.'

Fyfe could see their minds working. The questions came thick and fast. He and Munro were well practised in constructing sentences that sounded impressive but said nothing on close analysis. Everything was a possibility. Nothing had been ruled out. It was up to the Press to speculate and offer their own interpretation of events.

Munro brought the lively question and answer session to an end when the supply of pictures arrived. It had lasted more than an hour. The radio and television crews immediately moved in to corner them. They needed sound and vision bites apart from the actual conference. Munro took the radio reporters and went to find a quiet room away from the milling newspaper hacks checking the quotes in their notebooks. Fyfe led the camera crews up to the back of the lecture hall and watched them set up beside the window. On the other side of the glass tree branches shimmied silently back and forth in the blustery wind. He combed his hair and brushed dandruff from his shoulders as he prepared to repeat his statement and the bland replies to the same questions.

Outside it was very dark. He looked at his watch and realised he was going to be late collecting Jill and Number Five.

Sleeping dogs, he thought, can't be left to sleep for ever.

47

Angela stood with stiff starfish hands on either side of her head as the carnage raged around her. It all happened so fast she could not count the number of shots fired. She was transfixed, watching Adamson scrambling away and hearing the sudden crack of the shattering glass and the surrealistic music of the pinball machine. Then Adamson out of nowhere, hurling himself against Gus and knocking them both through the wall and into the swimming pool.

She remained standing rigidly in the games room. Slowly she wrapped her arms tightly round her body in a token gesture at self-defence. While Gus Barrie and Adamson fought to the death in the pool she was looking the other way, staring in deep fascination at the snooker table and the overflowing sacks of money on the green baize. Billy Jones lay on the floor, stone dead, with large crescents of shiny red blood ballooning like a child's fancy-dress wings from his sides. His head was to one side and his tongue was a disconcerting shade of bright blue. Sandy looked like a disused ventriloquist's dummy. He was sitting on his backside, propped up by a leg of the table, with his legs splayed out and his hands curled pathetically in his lap. His battered head drooped. His chin rested on a bib of blood. He wasn't breathing. The light canopy over the table swung slowly to and fro sweeping a silent wind of shadows over the three fat sacks and the cascading pile of pale, colourful banknotes.

Angela came out of the trance gradually. The pinball music slowed and stopped. The money was hers, she was thinking, all hers. If they were all dead, the money was hers and no one would know about it. Mike would have fulfilled his promise to make her rich and she would be free, no longer dependent on anyone. This was her chance. There would be no witnesses. It would be her secret. This was what she had been waiting for.

She turned and the pieces of broken glass crunched under her feet. The debris made an unstable surface as she walked to the poolside. Gus's body was on the bottom, distorted by the diffraction of the light, seeming to ripple and flex as if it was still alive. Adamson was hanging on to the side with one arm, his whitened face screwed up with the pain and effort involved. Blood leaked from him in a dark cloud that faded and dispersed in the water. He looked up at her and his eyes pleaded for help. He was holding on to the smooth, slippery surface with the flat of one hand. His other arm hung uselessly at his side. She knew he was at her mercy. Without her, his grip would give out and he would slip back into the water and drown.

'It wasn't the real money,' he sobbed, each word acting as a determined slap to his own face to keep him conscious. 'It wasn't from the robbery. Gus had it and he told me to tell you it was from the robbery. He gave me the sacks. It was so he could impress you. He wanted you to think it was the money Mike stole, but it wasn't. Mike burned it. He really did. Gus put this money together. It was his own money. It didn't have anything to do with me. I had never seen it before.'

Angela believed him. He was too far gone to lie and it all made perfect sense. What a sweetie Gus was to go to all this trouble for her. He was as mad as his brother Mike. All that money in untraceable notes. She would have been obliged to stay with him if he had survived. Poor Gus. Lucky Angela.

She stepped closer. This was her chance. No witnesses, she thought. It will be my secret. The sharp stiletto heel of her shoe stabbed down on to Adamson's hand. He snatched it away, sinking immediately, clutching once more at the side. She stamped on the hand again, grinding the heel down hard. Adamson cried out once but it was cut short as he slid under the water.

Angela stood on the edge of the pool. She held her breath as long as she could and then sucked in air in short rapid gasps. Adamson stayed below the surface, apparently curling into a tight ball at the bottom as if he was going to sleep.

He was dead. There were no witnesses. She was free.

When she heard the sound of footsteps behind her she didn't turn round. She froze. Muscles tightened painfully in her neck and legs. Silence screamed around her and then fled as the quiet sound of more footsteps circled round her.

'Well, well,' said a man's voice. 'Fancy meeting you here.'

48

David Fyfe stood at the limit of the tidal wave of glass shards and took in the scene in front of him. He saw the two obviously dead bodies beside the snooker table and slowly walked round to the other side of the swimming pool to look down on the other two dead bodies in the water.

Angela stood opposite him, looking tremendously vulnerable in her short black figure-hugging dress. He was not surprised to see her. She did not look up until he spoke. In the few seconds it took to raise her head he relived every intimate detail of the intense love affair that had briefly united them after Mike's death nine years before.

'David Fyfe as I live and breathe,' she said.

'Which is more than your friends do,' he replied, gesturing with a flick of his head.

Fyfe had not set out from police headquarters with the intention of going to Gus Barrie's. He had left a note on his door saying he had gone to eat and taken the car to collect Jill and Number Five from Catriona's. There he had drunk coffee from a Dennis the Menace mug and watched himself on television and tried to shake the niggling thought that Gus Barrie was the key to the slaughter going on in the city. So, reunited with his dogs, he decided to take a drive past the Barrie house because it wasn't that far and he had been there before to question Gus on a drug death case that was destined to go no further. At one point it had been believed there was enough evidence to charge him but Barrie had bluffed it out, never needing to consult the smart-alec lawyer hovering in the background all the time. A team of accountants could not pick holes in his money management system. In the end the evidence was far too circumstantial and no self-respecting fiscal would take it to court. Case closed.

The gates of Barrie's house were open. If they had been closed Fyfe would have turned round. Instead he drove in. Jill sat beside him on the front seat, staring ahead. He knew he was breaking all the rules, but he could not stop himself. He was acutely aware of the risk he was taking by coming alone. Who did he think he was? What did he think he was playing at? If Barrie was involved in the murders, an unarmed policeman with no back-up and no clear conception of what he was doing would hardly pose insurmountable problems. It would be better to forget this rash impulse, better to return to headquarters and share the information about the Transit van. Then he could join the snatch squad and descend on the house, sirens wailing.

The curve of the driveway disappeared into the tall, straight trees that lined each side. He would just look, he told himself. He would check the house from the outside. He would do no more than that.

A corner of the house came into view and then, as he rounded the bend, the whole frontage. The walls were floodlit. Glass gaped black to the touch of the light. Barrie's Jaguar was at an angle across the entrance, its wheels on full lock showing the fatness of the tyres and the scar lines of the tread.

Fyfe got out of his car. The dogs watched him go. Wood pigeons cooed above him. One took off, making him flinch as its wings beat their way through a curtain of thin branches. His heart was pounding furiously; not from fear but from the prospect of gross embarrassment if he was caught. How could he explain that he had come alone because unknown forces had summoned him to this spot? He had come because of the death of a suicidal old man, the out-of-character decision of a homosexual judge, and an encounter with a computer screen. That was the real reason he was outside the front door of a ruthless criminal. As a career move it was rather regressive. All that could be said for it was that his behaviour might help him get early retirement on health grounds.

If the door was locked, he told himself, he would turn round and leave. It was open. It allowed him to pass into the darkened hallway. As he entered, concealed lights at head height switched themselves on to illuminate the space he was in. There was no one to be seen, no sound to be heard. Fyfe straightened up, deciding to brazen it out and flash the warrant card as protection. He would worry about the propriety of it later. He set off down the dim hallway. The lights followed alongside, always keeping just a little in front.

He came to the brightly lit swimming pool area and marched straight in. A bear hug of apprehension enveloped his chest. It took him several seconds to work out that the water-thrown shadows were glittering and sparkling on piles of broken glass strewn all over the ground. He was shocked by his calmness in the presence of the death and destruction. He was unsurprised to see Angela dancing nervously at the edge of the swimming pool. It would all make perfect sense. That was why he had come. To help it make sense.

'It looks like you've had quite a party,' he said.

'Will it do any good to tell you none of this has anything to do with me? I didn't kill anyone. Can you believe it?'

'Probably. You and I were always honest with each other. Remember?'

'Oh yes. I remember.'

She launched into an explanation of events while he watched the bodies floating in the pool. One had its arms spread wide and the jacket flapped back like the cloak of a cartoon superhero. It was Barrie. Beyond it another body was lying on its side, its arms wrapped loosely round its knees. Its eyes were wide open. He recognised John Adamson. That's it then, he thought. Case closed.

'It was Gus that caused this,' Angela explained. 'He got me across from Spain with the promise that he would be recovering Mike's money. He was fixated on me, desperate for me to marry him. I came over because I was curious. I always knew the money was destroyed.'

'So did I,' Fyfe agreed.

'But Gus said it had been hidden away all this time and if I came over he would make Adamson get it for me. Just for me.'

Everything had flowed from Gus Barrie trying to buy Angela's affection by emulating his little brother. Father Quinn's downfall had been the calling in of debts to achieve the necessary liquidity. Father Byrne must have known about Adamson and the money and tried to get in on the act. The whole episode was shot through with deception but it all made sense.

Angela was waving at the sacks of money on the snooker table. Fyfe had not appreciated what it was before.

'They paraded Adamson in front of me,' she said. 'They were going to kill him but he fought back and they all ended up dead. All of them. I couldn't do anything. Poor Gus. He thought he was untouchable.'

Angela looked round, expecting more policemen to come rushing in. She seemed resigned to her fate. Fyfe had no crisis of conscience about rescuing her. It seemed the natural thing to do.

'Let's go,' he said. 'We can be out of here before the police arrive.'

'But you are the police, Dave.'

'I'm on a break. Do you want me to help you or not?'

'Are you alone?' She frowned in bewilderment.

173

'I work better that way.'

'You mean there are no other policemen outside?'

'Not a one. You and I are the only living souls here. Angela, this is your lucky day.'

'I always did like you, Dave.'

'It was mutual.'

They agreed she should get her clothes, that she should leave no trace of herself in the house. She would vanish into thin air. While she was up in the bedroom Fyfe tiptoed through the broken glass to stare in astonishment at the sacks of money.

49

Angela waited for Fyfe to say something in the car but he didn't. She wanted to know where he was taking her. She wanted to know why he was doing it. She wanted to know what he was going to do with the money. Most of all she wanted to know what he was going to do with the money. But he kept his eyes on the road, never looking at her, and there was a strangely ambivalent expression on his face, a mixture of surprise and amusement.

He had come up to the bedroom to help her with her heavy cases and she had fallen against him, making sure he appreciated the contact of their bodies. Her hands were on his shoulders, so close to him she could feel her warm breath deflected back against her own face. He appreciated it. His hands stroked the soft silver and black fur of her coat when he grabbed her waist to steady her. In the shifting bubble of light, she followed him along the corridors and down the stairs to the outside. The boot was stuffed with the sacks of money. Angela's cases had to go on the back seat, pushing the dog called Number Five into a corner. Jill lay at Angela's feet as they went down the driveway.

Instinctively, it felt right. Fyfe was no ordinary policeman who saw things in black and white, good and evil. More and more of their pillow talks came back to her. Even after nine years, she trusted Fyfe to look after her. Don't ask why. Act dumb and shy. Men liked her that way. There was no point in hiding, no point in resisting. Abject surrender was the only course left to her. She had been truthful with him up to a point. He hadn't seen her kick Adamson into the swimming pool and she hadn't told him, but she hadn't lied outright. If Fyfe had realised, things might be totally different. Her luck was holding.

Angela had thrown herself on his mercy and would soon know what she could get away with. She was good at that. She stroked Jill's head to show whose side she was on.

'You do believe me, don't you?' she asked finally, intimidated by the silence.

'Yes.'

'Why?'

'You're not really dressed for a fast getaway,' he said. 'You hadn't planned anything.'

Angela felt warm air begin to swirl about her bare legs. She pulled the fur coat more closely around her and it rode up over her thighs. The heat in the car crept up and over, making her drowsy. She had travelled a great distance. She was suddenly exhausted. She hardly noticed the streets they drove through, or the people they passed. When Fyfe stopped outside a row of terraced houses and stopped the engine she heard the rain pattering steadily on the car roof.

'Where are we?' she asked.

'A safe place.'

'Who lives here?'

'Nobody. That's what makes it safe.'

They got out of the car and hurried to the door. The dogs scampered after them. Angela stood so close to Fyfe he could not move his arm freely to turn the key. The lock was awkward. Always had been. He had never acquired the knack of working it first time.

'Aren't you coming in?' Angela said, grabbing at his arm when he held back on the threshold.

'I'm going to get your cases. Sorry about the mess inside, by the way. I've been meaning to decorate.'

The flat was almost but not quite unfurnished. Big rooms, high ceilings, cobwebs in the corners. In the living-room there were two armchairs. In the back bedroom there was a bed, a rocking chair and a gas fire that lit first time with a deep-throated whoomp. The wallpaper had been torn and scribbled on. Fyfe brought in the cases and dumped them on the bed. The dogs sniffed round the skirting boards.

'The last tenants did a moonlight flit,' he said. 'I'm going to buy you a ticket for the late sleeper. You'll be safe once you're out of the city.'

'How do I know you'll come back?' she asked.

'You can hold my dogs hostage. I have to go back to the office though. I'll be a couple of hours.'

Angela watched him drive away with her inheritance in the boot. There was nothing she could do to stop him.

50

Fyfe stopped at a hole-in-the-wall money machine. He was about to withdraw enough cash to buy a sleeper ticket to London when he remembered the sacks of money in the boot. He cancelled the transaction and helped himself to a handful of notes. He drove down the ramp into Waverley Station and parked diagonally nose-in to the kerb round from the ticket office. A yellow cleaning machine with a whining electric motor whirling brushes on both sides swept accumulated debris into a central gap at the front. The driver mounted on top of it was wearing a short-sleeved white shirt and a peaked cap pushed right to the back of his head. He picked a cigarette end from his mouth and flicked it on to the ground ahead so he could run over it and clean it up. Fyfe pulled up his collar like a private eye in a melodrama and went to buy a first class ticket in the name of Mrs Smith. The train was due to leave in four hours.

Back in the car Fyfe had to grip the steering wheel tightly to stop his hands shaking. The hairs on the back of his neck stood on end when he thought about the bundles of banknotes behind him. What was he doing? He had helped a prime murder suspect to escape from the scene of the crime. Not only that, but he had helped her get away with more than one million pounds in stolen money. What had possessed him to act so outlandishly? On first contact with Angela he had been so calm and collected, so sure of himself. Now he was a nervous wreck, horrified by what he had done but also, in a curiously detached way, proud of himself. Angela was no murderer. The money wasn't stolen. He was living in a cocoon of self-absorption, like the lights that followed moving bodies in Barrie's house of the dead. No one was moving there now, Fyfe thought. It was all silence and darkness.

He drove up the one-way ramp out of the station. There were drunks staggering about on the streets and hanging on to lampposts as though the city had been struck by an earthquake. The Scott Monument soared spectacularly above the trees of Princes Street Gardens. Moonlight glowed between its arches and flying buttresses like something out of a science fiction tale.

He had to return to headquarters. He had to show face. It wouldn't be an alibi but it was the sensible thing to do. His mind was operating independently, working out in best police officer fashion what he could do to minimise the chances of being caught. There was no way back. He couldn't turn Angela in or she would tell the whole story. How could he explain? Why would anyone install a woman in an empty flat and then buy a train ticket to London for her if he didn't intend to see her escape? Angela knew it too. She was dependent on him. He was dependent on her. They shared the new secret.

He parked his car and walked into the busy incident room, straight through to his office without hesitating. No one challenged him. No one asked him where he'd been for the previous two hours. No one seemed to have missed him.

Fyfe sat down and the back of the chair bounced off the wall. A new pile of interview reports had grown in the in-tray. He called up the Sleeping Dogs program and typed in the registration numbers again. Windfall Construction's name appeared on the screen. He lifted the phone and dialled Mark Munro's extension. It answered on the second ring. Fyfe told him about the old witch and the Windfall van being in the street outside the redhead's flat and its link to Gus Barrie.

'That's hard enough in my book,' Munro said. 'Worth a visit. What do you think?'

'It's a big company. A lot of vans. There could be a million reasons.'

'We can ask Gus to think of a few. It's time we rattled a few cages. How about you and me?'

'Tomorrow morning?'

'Seven. Just to keep Gus on his toes.'

'See you here at six thirty.'

'Okay, Dave.'

'I'm going to take this pile of reports home with me and sift through them to see if there's anything we need to know.'

'Right. See you tomorrow. Bright and early.'

'It will be a good start to the day. Trust me, Mark. I've got a good feeling on this one. We're on the right track.'

Fyfe held the interview reports under his arm and walked out, passing conversational remarks about the weather and what a long day it had been on the inquiry. He opened the boot of his car and slid the reports down the side of the bulging money sacks. No point in bothering to read them, he thought, slamming the lid.

Fyfe knew he was acting recklessly but he didn't care. Fatalism surrounded him like a winding sheet. The illicit thrill of joining the criminal class was nothing more than a hollow feeling in his stomach and maybe that was simple hunger because he had eaten hardly anything that day. He reasoned that if Sylvia could marry a queer judge to buck the system, why shouldn't he help a blameless victim of circumstance to do the same? Angela had done nothing wrong.

The real criminals were out of the game. Tomorrow would be a short day. Case closed before breakfast. Guaranteed. How was that for co-ordination?

51

Angela hid by the side of the window in the near-empty living-room and watched Fyfe's car stop outside the flat. He went straight to the boot and lifted out two of the sacks, one in each hand. Bundles of banknotes spilled from the neck of one and fell on to the road. She stepped in front of the window, making an involuntary grab at the notes through the glass. Fyfe crouched down and stuffed them back in with the rest. He paused to let a pedestrian pass before carrying the sacks over the pavement and up the steps to the door. Angela heard the key scraping in the lock. She saw the third sack lying in the open boot with the lid rocking in the wind. A group of three people passed by without a backward glance. 'He's gone mad,' she said. 'He'll have us both caught.'

She hurried through to where he was still trying to work the tricky lock and opened the door. He smiled, threw in one sack and kicked the other after it over the floor. Then he went to collect the other one.

Angela waited, staying back from the door. Since he had left her she had been prowling anxiously about the flat, her mood swinging erratically between resignation and resentment. Jill and Number Five followed her around for a while but quickly got bored and curled up in front of the fire in the stiflingly warm bedroom to sleep. She kept her fur coat on and moved around constantly in the chill air outside the bedroom worrying that Fyfe would turn her in. There was nothing she could do to stop him. He was the master of the instance. She was completely at his mercy.

She had mostly stood by the window and waited for him to return, remembering the torrid, clandestine affair that had developed between them nine years before. They had slept together for the first time on the morning of Mike's funeral. How had it happened? He was going on duty that afternoon and had come round early. She had given him a key. She had been startled to wake to see him standing over her. But then it seemed so natural that he should climb into the bed beside her and she could close her eyes and imagine he was Mike. And again, when Fyfe returned after midnight and she was sitting up waiting for him in her funereal black dress. There had been no arrangement. She willed him to appear. She remembered that they had never said much to each other, only inconsequential conversations among the slippery physical stuff. She had never understood how or why it had happened. But when it ended it seemed natural too. She willed him out of her life. Fyfe had served his purpose at the time. Now he was serving another purpose. He was being Mike again for her, finally delivering the reward promised so long ago.

Angela watched Fyfe bring in the third sack and dump it on top of the others. He closed the door, took something from his pocket and handed it to her. She studied the train ticket and smiled hugely.

'You really are going to help me get away, aren't you?'

'Did you ever doubt me?'

'Just a little. Why are you doing this?'

Fyfe didn't have a simple answer to that question. 'For old times' sake,' he said.

'Our old times didn't amount to much.'

'More's the pity.'

'When is the train?'

'Two hours from now.'

Angela took him by the arm and led him along the corridor into the bedroom. She had to keep him from thinking clearly. She had to make the time pass so that he could not have the chance to change his mind. The dogs came over to sniff at Fyfe's hand and went back to their places in front of the fire. She went ahead of him and turned back to face him.

'Did I tell you, Dave? I've been away from home a long time but I'm still just an old-fashioned Edinburgh girl at heart.'

'You are?'

'Oh yes. I've been away a while it's true but it never leaves you. You know what I mean, don't you, Dave? An old-fashioned Edinburgh girl is all fur coat...'

She switched off the light. The red glow of the gas fire rippled over the movement of the black and silver fur as it slipped off her shoulders to fall silently at her feet. Without hesitating she crossed her hands, took hold of the hem of her short dress and pulled it up over her head in a single motion. The dress joined the coat on the floor. She kicked off the high-heeled shoes and was completely naked in front of him.

'All fur coat,' she repeated, affectionately cupping the side of Fyfe's neck with the palm of one hand. 'And no knickers.'

She pushed him back on to the bed and fell on top of him. He hindered, rather than helped her frantic efforts to get his clothes off. Finally they had sex without exchanging another word. It did not take long. Angela remained on top, making all the right noises, her fingers interlocked with his, hair hiding her face. In the semi-darkness he turned his head to the side and watched the reflection in the mirror copying their every movement. When he arched his back he could see a fat full moon hanging through a gap in the curtains in the upper half of the streaming wet window. Its surface seemed to form the image of the bowed head of a long-haired woman looking down on him, standing out from its background like a profile on a cameo brooch. There were thin black bars on the window. When Fyfe blinked and refocused to try and see the moon more clearly they sliced the bright shining disc into strips.

Angela's hot breath touched his face and flowed over it like a liquid substance. Her hair covered his eyes and her mouth closed over his. The moon was eclipsed. The climax came with the new darkness, emptying him of all guilt and all doubts for as long as it lasted.

52

Fyfe dreamed of making love to Sylvia while Brother Patrick stood over them, arms folded into the opposite sleeves of his habit. As they broke apart and lay panting in the afterglow, the monk stole away soundlessly on his air-cushioned soles to be replaced by Angela's naked figure appearing out of the darkness and running towards him until she tripped and rose in the air to come plummeting down on top of him, hair streaming back, fingers like claws, teeth bared.

Fyfe opened his eyes. An instant of utter panic electrified him and his entire body tensed in anticipation of the imagined impact. Nothing happened. Slowly, he relaxed.

Angela was leaning on an elbow beside him staring into his face. Through the triangle formed by her arm he could see the mirror and himself and the straight line of her spine and the roundness of her buttocks. She continued to stare. One breast lay on his chest, a hand played idly along the inside of his leg.

'Why are you doing this for me?' Angela asked.

Fyfe tried to shrug his shoulders but it was impossible because he was lying on his back and she had him pinned to the bed. 'Why not?' he said.

'There has to be a reason,' she insisted. 'There has to be a reason why we're here together like this. Why you and I should be in this situation.'

'When you discover what it is let me know, will you?'

She shook her head, smiling, and her hand moved up his leg. 'Why are you doing this for me?' she asked again.

In the mirror Fyfe saw his hand caress the small of Angela's back, slowly following the smooth curve of her backside. They made love again much more slowly. Both of them kept their eyes open trying to stare the other out as the quietly building crescendo of biological passion became the only thing of importance.

He must have slept again, dreamlessly. The next thing he was aware of was lying on his back with Angela sitting on the edge of the bed, still naked, her back erect, applying make-up to her face. She turned her head, pouted with blood-red lips and blew him a shiny wet kiss. He snatched at the air to catch it.

'It's time to go,' she said. 'What are we going to do about the money?'

'It belongs to you, Angela.'

She did not look round. 'That's all right, then,' she said.

53

Angela dressed in a red blouse, black trousers and sensible shoes. Fyfe poured the banknotes into the three suitcases and put Angela's clothes into the empty sacks. There was just enough space in the cases for the swap-over. The dogs got excited, anticipating departure.

'Do you want a share?' Angela asked.

'I can't. I'm a policeman,' Fyfe said and almost burst out laughing. He was a fine, upstanding example of moral perfection and ethical behaviour. Who did he think he was kidding? He wasn't a white knight rescuing a damsel in distress. He was a selfish bastard, interested only in his own gratification. A little extra cash in hand wouldn't hurt. Maybe he would resign and live off it. Why not? It was a tempting proposition. He would find some way of explaining it to his wife.

'Are you sure?' Angela said.

'On second thoughts I wouldn't mind a little financial windfall. How much is there?'

'I haven't counted it.'

'Well, it's your money.'

'I wouldn't have it if it wasn't for you.'

'True enough.'

'Here. You take one suitcase, and I'll have the other two. Is that a deal?'

'Sounds fair to me. Easy come, easy go.'

'I couldn't have done it without you, Dave.'

The tall windows were all in darkness as they left, curtains pulled back and tied at the sides like sinister wraiths, backs to the wall, peering round the corner. Not a word was spoken during the short journey to the station. It was just before midnight and the city was hoaching with late-night drinkers. Fyfe realised that he was running the risk of being recognised but he made no attempt to hide or hurry. He was totally convinced everything was working out. The engagement party would be in full flow by now. Lord Greenmantle would be seated in his fireside chair with Sylvia standing at his shoulder, accepting the congratulations of their colleagues. John Adamson would never know he owed his freedom and his death to sexy Sylvia, Fyfe's sometime lover, who had taken the edge off the bad temper of a hanging judge at the opportune moment. If Greenmantle had stayed grouchy, Adamson would still be in prison and a lot of people would still be alive. Fyfe would still be a poor man.

Down the ramp into Waverley. Jill lay at Angela's feet. Number Five sat on the back seat. Fyfe parked the car and, without asking, heaved out the two bigger cases. He escorted Angela to the train. They found the compartment and checked in with the sleeper attendant. She went in first and he dumped the cases on the bunk.

'Will you be all right, Angela?' he asked.

'Thanks to you I will be.'

'Do you need anything?'

'I can get by.'

'Look me up the next time you're passing through. I'm in the book. Dial 999.'

'I don't know where I'll end up.'

'Send me a postcard.'

He turned to go but she grabbed his shoulder. 'You're not going to leave without kissing me goodbye, are you?'

'Since you asked so nicely.'

They kissed, long and slow, and he left. Dozens of people were saying their farewells on the platform. Fyfe wondered absently if he and Angela would ever meet again. She would be down on her knees in the compartment now, counting her money. He would go back and count his.

Already he could see his immediate future scrolling ahead of him. The visit to Gus Barrie's to discover the murder scene. He would grind some broken glass into the soles of his shoes, touch things unnecessarily to leave prints. The piecing together of events would be a difficult exercise over the course of the day. Fyfe would be sceptical, hard to convince. Was it not possible somebody else could be involved? No evidence. Maybe not. He would slowly allow himself to be persuaded. Everything would be accounted for. All the loose ends would be tied up nicely, the package wrapped and stored away. An announcement would be made that no one else was being sought in connection with the inquiry. Case closed.

Fyfe was not afraid of being found out. His policeman's intuition told him he was on a winner. Only two people in the world knew what had happened. He was one of them. Angela was the other and she would never tell. They understood each other so well. It was their secret. Another intimacy they shared.

He was a real criminal now, beyond the pale, a survivor of invisible armed robbers, of corrupt priests who fell off cliffs and monks sneaking around noiselessly in white Reeboks, of pale-skinned redheads lying dead and a grinning judge in red robes with a blonde on his knee and a pardon in his hand, of cold-eyed gangsters and a swimming pool full of bloody water, of a sexy old friend in a fur coat and nothing else. There were no rules in the book to extricate him from this situation. Strange how he didn't feel any different from the day before.

He would decide on a suitable hiding place for his share of the booty, somewhere simple like behind the cold water tank in the loft. And he would have an endless ready supply of spending cash. Maybe he would stick a bundle in a brown paper envelope and send it north to Brother Patrick. He would definitely compose a resignation letter to Hunky Dunky and carry it around with him for use whenever the feeling came over him. He estimated there was maybe two hundred thousand pounds in the suitcase if he was lucky. What a fool he was. If he was going to be a criminal he might as well be a rich one. The original robbery had netted well over one million. He could have had double the amount he had settled for so easily. He should have taken half. He still could. The train was still at the platform. He hesitated, turned and looked back. No. The moment had passed. There could be no going back now. It was a different time. A different world.

Sally would arrive back the next morning, probably at the same platform. He would be there to carry her cases to the car.

'How was your weekend?' she would ask.

'Nothing special,' he would reply.

In the car Jill was sitting behind the steering wheel and Number Five was beside her on the passenger seat. He climbed in and shooed them away. Number Five jumped in the back. Jill went to her usual spot below the dashboard and turned round three times. Before he had started the engine both had heads on front paws and eyes closed.

'Sleep peacefully, my bairns,' he said quietly. 'Sleep well.'

Printed in Great Britain
by Amazon